O'Connell's Treasure
a MIKE4 Novel

Readers are encouraged to go to www.MissionPointPress. com to contact the author or to find information on how to buy this book in bulk at a discounted rate.

Published by Mission Point Press
2554 Chandler Rd.
Traverse City, MI 49696
(231) 421-9513
www.MissionPointPress.com

ISBN: 978-1-950659-38-8
Library of Congress Control Number
available upon request

Printed in the United States of America

O'CONNELL'S TREASURE

J.R. SEEGER

BOOK 4 IN THE MIKE4 SERIES

MISSION POINT PRESS

There are no absolute rules of conduct, either in peace or war. Everything depends on circumstances.

—Leon Trotsky

CONTENTS

>>>>>> **PROLOGUE**

I t was a simple mission.

Hauptmann Jan Steinmark sat with his three commandos in the rear deck next to a dinghy hanging from the davits of the disguised German Navy vessel. Hundreds of miles to the south and east, Afrika Corps Commander General Erwin Rommel intended to flank the British forces and capture Tobruk. Rommel needed the best possible intelligence on British land, sea and air forces. When German commanders needed intelligence and needed it quickly, they used the commando element of German intelligence known as the Brandenburg Division. Tonight, Steinmark's team was that element using guile, audacity and a little luck to acquire the intelligence.

The mission required the team to infiltrate by sea to the Palestinian coast on a moonless night. Their goal was to capture codes and, with luck, a prisoner from a British Navy signals station at Jaffa on the Palestinian coast. They would return to the coast 24 hours later to be picked up by a submarine. As the modified fishing trawler sailed silently toward the coast, Steinmark thought about the good fortune that brought him to this mission, far away from the meatgrinder of the Eastern Front.

Before he had time for his reminiscences, the chief petty officer for the boat came down from the pilot house and said, "Ten minutes to station, Sir." Steinmark nodded and looked at the radium dial of his watch. The lieutenant in charge might look like he still belonged in school, but he had navigated the course perfectly. They should be right on time for their rendezvous on the Palestinian shore.

The Brandeburger's missions often employed captured British vehicles and uniforms along with clandestine delivery from the sea by boat or submarine. In this case, infiltration was courtesy of another Brandenburger team running a small fleet of craft out of Rhodes. The boats looked like any of the other Greek and Turkish fishing vessels that still worked in the Eastern Mediterranean, but this one was modified to include two large diesel engines cannibalized from a damaged E-boat. That meant the boat was fast. The boat also had the new *Seetakt*, that used electromagnetic signals to identify ships. Steinmark was an engineer by training, but he barely understood how radio signals could be bounced off objects and deliver an accurate location of the enemy well outside the range of the most powerful Kriegsmarine binoculars. The lieutenant simply said the *Seetakt* made their job of infiltration and evasion much easier. The boat could deliver a team along the Egyptian and Palestinian coast from their base in Rhodes and disappear into the night.

It wasn't the first time Steinmark and his three trusted companions had gone behind British lines, but it was the first time they needed a guide. Steinmark knew a guide was a potential source of compromise. Local agents were susceptible to British security services just as the British agents in France or the Soviet agents in Poland were targets of their German counterparts.

"Sir, do you know the guide?" Oberfeldwebel Schmidt's comment reflected his own concerns.

"Schmidt, I only know what we were told. A local resistance fighter. Tired of living under British rule. He has a reputation for delivering good intelligence."

"And if he takes us into a trap, he will have seen his last sunrise."

Steinmark nodded and said, "Exactly so."

The approach went as planned. In the dead of night, the trawler dropped anchor less than 100 meters from shore and the trawler's crew dropped the dinghy silently into the water. The four-man team went over the side into a wooden dinghy and two sets of oars quietly slipped into the water as the commandos pulled toward the beach. The men wore the deck uniform of the German submarine fleet: Dark blue wool and black wool knit caps. No insignia revealed their rank or unit. Only their weapons showed German affiliation: Schmeisser machine pistols, "potato masher" hand grenades, a German panzer-faust anti-tank grenade launcher, and a German field pack filled with explosives.

The team left the dinghy on the surf line and walked onto the beach. The row boat would float out to sea with the tide and disappear. After the mission, a German submarine would send in inflatables two miles further down the beach to pick up the team and, with luck, a British prisoner. Steinmark checked his dive watch. 0200hrs local. He was pleased with the precision so far. They were on time and in the right location. All they needed now was to linkup with their Palestinian guide and head to their target.

The spotlight from the British jeep in the ambush position bathed the team in white light.

British Tommies in their distinctive helmets were standing in formation to either side of the light. In the shadow of the light, Steinmark could see the Tommies, their rifles with bayonets attached, standing in parade formation. A megaphone voice called out of the darkness: "All right then, gentlemen. The game is up. Raise your hands." In that moment, Steinmark thought "They just expect us to surrender as if we were villains caught robbing a bank. As if this was some sort of movie. They are children in this type of war." If Steinmark had been in charge of the ambush, he would have issued no warning and none of the team would have survived the first ten seconds of gunfire.

Instead, Steinmark made it clear to the Tommies that they were wrong to assume the commandos would surrender. He used the first burst from his machine pistol to shoot out the spotlight. To his right, Oberfeldwebel Schmidt tossed a smoke grenade followed by an anti-personnel grenade in front of the ambushers. To his left, Feld-webel Braunfels tossed a second anti-personnel grenade. Before the second grenade exploded and by the time the Tommies had recovered their night vision, Steinmark and his men were down the beach running for their lives. Schmidt had worked the team hard during rehearsals for *actions on contact*. His training saved them from initial capture or death. Now it was up to Steinmark's leadership to evade the Tommies and get off the beach. That wouldn't be easy.

Schmidt was the consummate professional NCO and had trained them mercilessly, but it was Steinmark who demanded they take the *panzerfaust* on the mission. Stealth was the Brandenburger trademark and Schmidt couldn't imagine why they would need an anti-tank weapon. Steinmark was certain that if they had trouble, that trouble would think twice after receiving the killing end of a German anti-tank rocket. He had seen the panicked response of Soviet infantrymen in the Eastern Front when they faced an in-bound rocket headed toward any nearby T34 tank or bunker. Panic was predictable when the anti-tank round exploded in front of you, destroying your night vision. As soon as the team reached the first set of dunes away from their landing site, he instructed Feldwebel Mathias to load and fire the *panzerfaust* at the jeep. The anti-tank grenade exploded in a flash of white light sending its shaped charge through the engine, into the passenger space and distributing shrapnel everywhere as the round exited near the rear tire.

Even before the round exploded, they retreated for another 100 meters, and reached a dune closer to the water. The trawler had been watching the fight from the sea and had used the E-boat engines to move up the coast and as close to the surf line as they could risk. The team on the boat pulled the canvas from a quad-barreled anti-aircraft gun in the aft deck position and opened up on the British. This was no longer a clandestine encounter; it was now a full-fledged fire fight with the British suddenly facing the greater firepower. Under this new covering fire, the team entered the surf line and started to swim for the boat. Schmidt was hit as he left the beach. Mathias helped his senior NCO swim to their rescue ship.

Steinmark was the last man off the beach. In a final effort to dissuade the remaining pursuers, he set off a small charge that was intended for use when they arrived at their objective. The charge, a mix of plastic explosive and jellied gasoline, was designed to create a highly volatile fire inside the target. Exploding in the open, it threw burning jellied gasoline in all directions. The closest of the British troops were caught in the wall of flame. The charge did one other job. It burned the right side of Steinmark's face including his right eye.

With the commandos aboard, the trawler retreated into the darkness, spreading a long smoke trail and opening up the two German diesel engines to full throttle. They were out in the open sea before the British troops could call for a Navy patrol boat. By the time they reached Rhodes, Oberfeldwebel Schmidt had died from his wounds and Steinmark had lost the use of his right eye. It was not a proper end to his year in Brandenburg Division but Steinmark had seen enough combat to know the randomness of war. Sometimes the best soldiers died, while the weakest soldiers survived to be hailed as heroes.

>>>>>> PARATROOPER

Operation Husky. 09 July 1943

Captain Peter O'Connell looked out of the jump door on the left side of his C47 Dakota heading toward the Sicilian coast. His stick of paratroopers from the third battalion of the 504th Parachute Infantry Regiment were going to Gela to support the allied invasion of Italy. They were part of a mission of the 82nd Airborne Division to conduct disruption behind the German lines. The allied commanders hoped the disruption would reduce the German Army's ability to defend the beaches of Sicily. This was the first US airborne operation in Europe and could mean the difference between success and failure for the invasion force. The sky around them held dozens of aircraft filled with paratroopers and dozens of Dakotas towing gliders with more soldiers and equipment headed to Sicily. It was also O'Connell's first combat jump and on a personal level he was determined to get his part of it right.

As jumpmaster, it was O'Connell's responsibility to make sure his paratroopers jumped at the right place and the right time. The pilot and crew chief might turn on the green light to signal it was time to go, but only O'Connell would lead the way. He leaned against the left side of the open cargo door, pushed his head further out into the slipstream, and looked toward the coast. Just forward of the engine, he could see a dozen other Dakotas traveling in what was called a V of Vs. He could also see the coast approaching. The crew chief tapped O'Connell on his right shoulder. He was wearing green coveralls, a leather flight jacket, and a headset linked by a long cable to the cockpit.

He shouted into O'Connell's ear. "Sir, pilot says one minute." O'Connell took another look down the length of the fuselage and he could see white surf breaking on the beach. He gave the crew chief a nod and gently pushed him away from the jump door. He wanted no one in the way of his paratroopers as they rushed out the door. During training, O'Connell came to realize that once the green jump light was on, nothing would stop paratroopers from exiting the aircraft. Nothing, including a crew chief who might be too close to the door. If all went well, the seventeen men in his stick would exit the aircraft in less than 15 seconds and would land together in an area the size of a football field. O'Connell knew from training that they would land together only *if* all went well.

He turned back into the aircraft, raised both hands with his index fingers extended and shouted as loud as he could over the noise of the engines. "One minute!" His paratroopers were already in line, using their right hands to balance against the skin of the aircraft and holding yellow static lines in their left hands. The opposite end of the static line was attached to a cable that ran the length of the aircraft. While they called it a "parachute jump," the truth was combat loaded paratroopers simply fell out the door when the light turned green. The parachute pack was only part of their load which included weapons, ammunition, some explosives, at least one or two knives, water and rations for at least two days. All told, each paratrooper carried well over 50 pounds of weight in addition to their parachute.

The aircraft made a hard-right bank just as O'Connell was returning to his position at the door. The motion almost tossed him to the opposite side of the aircraft. He caught his balance by grabbing the jump door frame. "Pilots are such jerks," he thought as he pulled himself back into the viewing position to determine the drop zone. What he saw instead was a wall of tracer rounds coming up from the ships off the coast. The pilots weren't jerks, they were just trying to dodge the wall of fire coming at the fleet of Dakotas flying the 82nd Airborne into the battle.

O'Connell shouted into the slipstream to no one in particular. "Shit. Our Navy is shooting at us!" He saw the lead aircraft in the first V of Vs formation receive a hit in one of the engines and the fuel tanks in the wing burst into flame. Paratroopers from that aircraft started jumping out. O'Connell could see they were too far from the coast. He understood why they were jumping, but he was certain they would not survive a water landing. With the weight they were carrying and covered by sinking parachute silk, there was scant hope of survival. Still, it was better than staying in a burning aircraft as it tumbled to earth.

He turned back to his stick. "Stand in the door!" He turned back and grabbed the doorframe with both hands. He felt the next man push tight against his parachute pack. Meanwhile, the aircraft again banked first to the left and then to the right and back to the left. O'Connell's grip on the door was weakened but he was determined — no matter what — to exit only once he could see they were over land.

Bang, bang, bang, bang. A sound like a nail being driven into a tin can. The aircraft was being hit by the tracer fire. O'Connell looked back into the darkened interior. No one was hurt but he could see more holes in the aircraft now as the cannon rounds went through the aircraft. O'Connell looked out the door and straight down between his jump boots. The beach was passing under his feet. Still a distance from the DZ, but if he had to, he could lead the stick out the door now. An explosion rocked the plane hard to the left and O'Connell was tossed out the door. His stick followed him.

"One, one thousand; two, one thousand; three, one thousand;...," O'Connell counted as he fell out of the sky. At airborne school, they made you say it out loud during every drill. If you got to five, you were supposed to pull your reserve parachute. He never made it to four one thousand which was a good thing because at jump altitude of 600 feet, it only took six seconds of freefall to hit the ground. A reserve parachute might or might not save your life in that last one hundred feet. This jump was no different from any of his previous jumps. Just as he shouted the number three, the opening shock of the parachute drove the air out of his lungs and dragged his crotch up to his chest. It wasn't pleasant, but it meant his parachute was open. He looked up at the green canopy; it was sound. He looked around. His seventeen paratroopers were in the sky around him. In the distance, he saw his aircraft banking hard and away from the beach. The port engine was on fire, but the fire didn't look to be spreading to the wing fuel tanks. No telling if the Dakota and crew would make it back to Africa.

For the first time since he exited the aircraft, O'Connell looked down at the ground. At this jump altitude, there wasn't much time on the descent to worry about where you were going to land. Still, he could see that he was drifting toward the Mediterranean. Not a good plan, so he pulled the two canvas risers attached to the harness on his right shoulder all the way to his chest. Months of pull-ups gave him the strength to pull and hold as the parachute slowly responded to O'Connell's efforts to change the parabolic shape of the parachute. His parachute slipped to his right, taking him away from the water and toward a cliff face overlooking the beach. Not an ideal landing spot but it would have to do.

"Hunnhmh." The landing drove the air from O'Connell's lungs and the parachute began to drag him along the ground toward the cliff face and the sea. "I am not going into the water tonight!" O'Connell said to himself as he used the canopy release assembly on his left shoulder to collapse the parachute. He then used the disc shaped chest release to clear himself of the harness. He rolled over on his stomach to catch his breath. At airborne school, the instructors taught you to stay in the prone position for a moment, just to be sure no one was shooting at you before you got up and moved to the fight. At this point, O'Connell wasn't entirely certain where the fight was. But there were no bullets flying overhead and no gunshots to be heard, so he decided it was time to get up, get his Garand rifle out of its canvas weapons case and assemble his paratroopers and start killing Germans.

"Welcome to Italy, Captain!" O'Connell looked to his right to see his First Sergeant walking to see if he was okay. First Sergeant Terry Tannenbaum was tall and lean. "A fence post with arms" was how the Battalion Sergeant Major described Tannenbaum. It hardly mattered to O'Connell what Tannenbaum looked like. He was one of the earliest volunteers for parachute training. He was also a graduate of the British commando school in Scotland. He never seemed to have anything but a smile on his face no matter how serious the situation. If anyone was going to keep O'Connell alive in Sicily, it was his first sergeant.

"Top, did your stick exit okay?"

"If you mean, did we all get out before our aircraft was shot to shit, yes sir. We all made it. I know the flyboys in my bird didn't."

"What the hell was the Navy thinking?"

"They were thinking we were Germans about to bomb them, sir. Scared kids sitting off the beach in their little boats. We'll see how that gets reported up the chain of command."

"OK, Top. Let's get our guys assembled and see if we can start a fight someplace on this island."

"Airborne, sir." They both walked away from the cliff face assembling soldiers from their own company and any other company they could find. They were nowhere near the planned drop zone. They knew the Germans were out there and they would find them and fight them, ideally before dawn. As they walked, O'Connell's First Sergeant fixed the bayonet to his Garand rifle and said to his young captain, "Sir, you never know when you are going to need your bayonet."

They worked through the early morning hours trying to find their men. O'Connell and Tannebaum quickly found a dozen paratroopers from their company and with that fighting force, they headed inland. As they did, they found other members of the 504th though not from their company. The paratroopers joined them and, by dawn, they had the equivalent of one platoon.

They had assembled near a stone fence line two miles from the drop zone. Paratroopers being mostly kids, they sat along the fence line and started eating from one of their two ration packs.

O'Connell said, "Top, what do you think? Do we just start the fight or continue to round up our guys?"

"Sir, my guess is that we aren't going to have much success finding more guys anytime soon. I reckon we just get started, but that's your call."

"They didn't send us here to round up strays. So, let's go find some Germans."

As O'Connell climbed over the fence, to his right he heard the sound of a German machine gun opening fire. In training command had exposed the 504th to the different sounds of American, British and German weapons. The regimental training sergeant said, "Men, we are going to fight in the dark. We need to know the sound of friendly weapons and enemy weapons. If they are friendlies, we go help. If they are enemy weapons, we run to the sound of the guns and take the fight to them." At the time, O'Connell thought it was a pretty corny instruction. In the current confusion, he understood. Paratroopers don't have the luxury of battle lines or trenches that tell them where the enemy is located. Paratroopers have to run to the guns.

"Gents, it's time to fight. Let's go." O'Connell headed toward the shooting. Behind him a rag tag group of young paratroopers dropped their food, stood up and followed. Tannenbaum pushed the last paratrooper over the wall. O'Connell could hear his first sergeant controlling their formation, fanning the men out in to a V formation, and telling each soldier to fix his bayonet.

As they crested a small hill, they finally saw what they had been hearing. Fifty yards to their front, four paratroopers were pinned down near another low stone wall facing a squad of German troops deployed from a half tracked armored personnel carrier. At the front the carrier, a German soldier was using a heavy machine gun to tear holes in the wall while a dozen of soldiers in field gray uniforms advanced. O'Connell turned to Tannebaum and said, "Who's the best shot here?"

"Sullivan."

"Get him up here and have him pick off the machine gunner. Once he does that, we open fire on the German squad. Let the guys know, our guys are behind that wall. No one shoots close to the wall."

"Check. Sullivan, get your nasty ass up here." Sullivan arrived. His shooting skills meant that he was issued a bolt action Springfield rifle with a telescopic scope. Not much more than the sort of scope used by deer hunters in the states, but it would give him a better chance of hitting targets at longer ranges. "The machine gunner, son. Take him out."

Sullivan nodded. He set up in the prone position, took aim and fired. His first round hit six inches below the machine gunner on the armor plate of the half track. The noise of machine gun must have masked the noise of the round hitting the carrier. Tannenbaum was watching with a pair of field glasses that probably belonged in a war museum. He said, "You missed, knucklehead. You were six inches below the gunner. Raise your point of aim ten inches."

Sullivan responded immediately with another shot. The round hit the German in the neck. He dropped like a stone. The gun stopped firing. The German troops advancing on the wall looked back at their fire support. O'Connell shouted, "Let them have it."

Twenty Garand rifles opened up at once sending rounds into the Germans. The remaining Germans who survived this initial barrage realized they had been flanked and, in good order, moved back to the half track carrier. This allowed the four paratroopers to finally open fire on the retreating Germans. Only two Germans were left when they got to the carrier. One was obviously the driver. He started the big German diesel, backed up the track and headed away from the fight. Sullivan used his rifle to sight in the driver as the half track pulled away. He fired again and Tannebaum saw the driver slump over the wheel. He watched as the half track drove into a small pond associated with the local farm.

O'Connell's first fight was over. He looked at his men, some he had never met before. They were a mix of seventeen and eighteen year olds. It was no wonder that they called him "the old man." At twenty one he must have seemed old and Tannenbaum at thirty must have seemed ancient. He looked at these kids who had just killed their first men and survived their first fight. They looked relieved and excited like kids who just won a football game. Tannenbaum solved that quickly. "Get up you mopes! You haven't won the war yet. Let's get down to see if we have any prisoners and to see if those four troopers are okay. Hurry up!"

O'Connell responded to his first sergeant's commands and led his small band of paratroopers to the field below. He realized later that he was relieved when he saw the Germans were all dead. He had no idea how to take prisoners when you were wandering behind enemy lines. The four paratroopers behind the wall were also relieved to be alive. Tannenbaum checked them to be sure there were no injuries and then told them they were now part of *his* company. As the sun started to beat down on his steel helmet, O'Connell smiled. He realized long ago that he might be the company commander but Tannenbaum owned the company.

The aide knocked on Donovan's office door. "Sir, there is a guy out here who insists he needs to see you."

"James, is it the President? Otherwise, I am pretty busy."

A deep voice from behind the door reached into the office. It sounded like a person who had spent his life shouting. "I'm not the goddamn President, but you better let me in, son, or the Colonel is going to see some broken furniture flying into his office along with your sorry young ass."

Donovan smiled. This was not the first time he had heard a voice from his past demanding an audience. "James, please let First Sergeant Patrick O'Connell into the office and get us a couple of mugs of cocoa. " A puzzled James Santini shrugged and turned sideways allowing the visitor into Brigadier General William J. Donovan's office. Donovan got up from behind his large oak desk and walked toward the door. Donovan knew his personal presence was imposing and especially now that he worked in a well-tailored general officer's uniform. But was not in his nature to reach across his desk to shake hands with an old comrade.

A square man with a square face and an ill-fitting black suit entered the office. In his early fifties, Patrick O'Connell hadn't changed much in stature from the last time Donovan saw him in Buffalo. He still looked like he could lift Donovan and his oak desk above his head with little difficulty. "Colonel, thanks for seeing me. Oh, sorry. General."

"Patrick, it didn't look like you were giving me much choice. How in the world did you get to DC? Don't you still live in Buffalo?"

"Sir, you know full well that since we got back from the war, I've worked for the New York Central. Fireman first, now an engineer. A good, steady job with a few benefits and a pension. We lived pretty well through the depression; not a lot of stuff but enough food on the table for the family. Right now, the best benefit is my railroad pass that gets me on trains anywhere in the system. I gave my seat to a sailor going home to NY City before shipping out, so I got here by riding in the cab with the train crew."

Santini brought in two white ceramic mugs of extra sweet cocoa. O'Connell shook the general's hand with a grip of iron.

"Patrick, you look fit, but, damn, you look old."

"General, hard work inside a locomotive will do that to you."

"So, why are you here, old son? I have a war to fight."

"That's why I'm here, Colonel. I want you to help my son help you fight your war. I'm sure the Army is good and all that, but it is a big outfit and from what I heard about the fighting in North Africa, some of our officers out there aren't up to the standards we had. I want my son to be working for the best guy I know. That's you, Colonel. I want him to fight for you."

O'Connell left only after Donovan promised to reach out to the 504th and see if Peter O'Connell would volunteer. He reminded O'Connell that the OSS was an all-volunteer outfit and if young Peter chose not to volunteer, then that was that. Patrick O'Connell took the General's hand and thanked him and walked out the door.

As soon as he did, Santini came in to collect the mugs and respond to any further tasking from Donovan. He said, "Sir, what was that all about?"

"James, in this life, you will learn to succeed through trading favors as much as you will succeed from hard work. Patrick O'Connell just called in at least one favor, probably two that I owe him from the Great War. The good news is I suspect we will end up gaining plenty from our end of the bargain. Please send a dispatch to our field recruiter in London, Major Bill Dennings. I promised O'Connell I would give his son a chance to become one of our glorious amateurs."

Donovan had Santini bring him another cup of cocoa. Alone again in his office, Donovan's mind wandered back a quarter of a century, to another war. It was a war that changed his mind completely about what it meant to win or lose and how to defeat an implacable enemy. With the OSS, he was building an organization that could collecting and delivering strategic intelligence to inform theatre commanders, an organization conducting attacks behind enemy lines, and an organization that was undermining enemy morale through targeted propaganda operations. None of these options were part of *his* war, sometimes called *The Great War,* but what Donovan knew was a savage war.

21 September 1918. AEF trenches, Ardennes, France

It was raining, again, and the troops in the trenches were soaked. Donovan walked among the troops in the companies of the 1st Battalion of the 165th Regiment of the 42nd Division of the American Expeditionary Force in France. This was the Buffalo unit of the New York National Guard historic "Fighting 69th" regiment made up of Irish troops from the state. He joined as a cavalry officer well before the US entered the Great War, but he arrived in France as an infantry Major. Six months later, as Lieutenant Colonel, he was commanding his battalion in the trenches. As he walked, he could hear the US artillery firing at the Germans and see the sky turn bright yellow as the rounds exploded less than a mile away. The fire was not concentrated or sustained, so Donovan knew it was not the preparation for an attack. The artillery fire was designed to keep the Germans off balance. So far, it seemed to have worked.

Donovan had already seen more combat than most officers of his rank. Trench warfare was close combat and fought in sprints across the line. Captains led their companies and battalion commanders watched from the trench lines preparing reserves to reinforce the attack as necessary. Donovan didn't follow those rules. He was not that sort of officer and as a result, he irritated virtually every senior in his chain of command. He had gone "over the top" multiple times as battalion commander and received a serious leg wound, gas injuries and medals to prove that he was not the normal field grade officer.

Donovan was not necessarily a brave man, but he thought that soldiers needed to see that their commanders were going to be there in the thick of it with them. If the thick of it meant blood, so be it. Today, the thick of it meant mud.

As he slogged along the muddy trench, Donovan knew he was losing as many men to illness and artillery shrapnel injuries as close combat. He was impatient to move forward and get the job done. As he walked past a company dugout in the trenches, a voice rang out.

"Colonel, you are going to get soaked if you don't start wearing the issued wool coats. I know they don't look very stylish, but you need to keep warm. And, by the way, if you don't change your socks, you aren't going to be able to walk the line. Get in here, dry off, and change your socks!"

Donovan recognized the voice of First Sergeant Patrick O'Connell, acting commander of Charlie company in his battalion. O'Connell's company commander was killed a month ago and O'Connell kept the company running as well as any in the Regiment. Donovan offered him a commission and O'Connell refused. Along with everything else, O'Connell volunteered for every scouting mission looking for routes in front of his company through the barbed wire and shell holes. He regularly reported to Donovan and his staff after a journey into no man's land, charcoal covered face and black wool watch cap on his head, a shotgun with a bayonet attached at his side. Donovan faced regular chastisement every time he walked by this company dugout representing the infantrymen from his hometown of Buffalo, NY. "Sir, we also have hot tea. Well, sort of."

Donovan passed through the tarp entrance and into the company dugout lighted by a single candle. Leaning against the wall were two Springfield rifles and a short barreled Winchester "trench" shotgun. All three had bayonets attached. Donovan leaned his Enfield next to the three weapons. In front of him stood O'Connell and his company runner Josh McKay. Donovan noticed McKay was out of breath. He must have seen Donovan walking the lines on the right flank and hurried to let his company commander know that the colonel was on the prowl. O'Connell handed Donovan a cup of tea (most probably strained through a no longer functional sock) and a tin of sugar. Donovan took both, put sugar in the tea and sat down on the only stool in the dugout.

"Sir, the next step is socks. Unwrap your puttees, get those boots off, take off your socks, wipe down those toes and put these on." O'Connell handed him a torn t-shirt to serve as a towel and a brand new pair of hand knitted socks. "Just got fifty pairs from the Buffalo Irish maidens determined to keep our toes attached to our feet." Donovan had noted trench foot was disabling about ten percent of his command every week, though not a single casualty from O'Connell's company. Now, he knew why.

"Fifty pairs, Patrick. That's not enough for the company."

"Colonel, we get about fifty pairs every two weeks. I arranged it through St. Joseph's Cathedral. It takes about two months to get them, but once the shipments started, we have had them every two weeks. I suspect every grandma in Buffalo is knitting socks now. Now are you going to take off those boots or do I have to order McKay to do the needful?"

Donovan took off his soaking puttees, nothing more than canvas wraps around his calves, and then his equally wet boots. Finally, he took off his cotton socks. They tore as he pulled them off.

"Colonel, hasn't anyone told you cotton kills in this environment? You need good wool socks. Put these on, try to dry them out each night. Here is a second set that you need to put in your pocket. Good feet, good soldier. You know better."

Donovan looked at the square Irishman with his tin pot cocked on the back of his head. He knew for certain that O'Connell was doing everything he could to make sure his company was ready to kill Germans when his time came to go over the top.

10 August 1943 – Sicily - 504th Parachute Infantry

Regiment Headquarters

Peter O'Connell had no idea why he had been summoned to regimental headquarters. The fight in July had been successful. He and his first sergeant had assembled as many paratroopers they could find and immediately started combat operations behind the German lines. He had been told that the work of the 82nd made a difference as the troops landed on the beaches. The fight for Sicily lasted a few more weeks as his paratroopers became light infantrymen working side by side with the other US and British infantry. Now, what was left of his company was living under green canvas on the edge of an airfield in the North end of the island awaiting further orders. Rumor was that their next stop was somewhere on the Italian West Coast, but no one knew when or where.

Normally, orders came by way of a unit briefing in another large tent. The chain of command meant that the 82nd Airborne Division commander briefed the regimental commanders and, in turn, they briefed their battalion commanders. A company commander would get his part of the order from his battalion commander. This time the regimental runner had come into O'Connell's company tent and asked for him to report to the Regiment command tent. The most terrifying part of the instruction was that O'Connell was to report alone. Any trip to the Regiment for a captain was likely not to be a good trip. O'Connell had met the Regiment's commander, Colonel

Rueben Tucker, only in large meetings as one of the many officers and senior enlisted men who made up the command group. One on one with the Regimental Commander suggested an ass chewing for something and O'Connell couldn't think what it was. Before he left the company tent, he asked Tannenbaum if he had any word of trouble from the Sergeant Major. He said no, but that didn't make O'Connell feel better.

When he entered the commander's office inside the tent, O'Connell immediately felt underdressed in his cotton combat uniform and carrying his steel pot under his left arm. Tucker was in his garrison uniform of green wool trousers and a tan wool shirt with a tan tie. O'Connell mostly focused on the silver eagles on Tucker's collar underscoring Tucker was a full colonel with all the authority he needed in wartime to do whatever he pleased with a young Captain with not quite two years in the Army. Tucker sat on a green folding chair in front of the small wooden field desk that fit into the trailer of his command jeep. The jeep and trailer, along with the field desk and the tent itself, arrived in Sicily by glider. Tucker arrived by parachute like everyone else in his command. On the canvas walls of the tent were maps of Sicily and central Italy. Another folding table to Tucker's right held aerial reconnaissance photos of German positions that O'Connell assumed were somewhere on the Italian coast.

Sitting to the left of Tucker was an Army major also in garrison uniform. There was a heavy leather flying jacket listing to the right on his folding chair and the major looked at least ten years older than Tucker. The flying jacket suggested the Major was from the Army Air Corps. However O'Connell had learned to pay attention to what a senior officer wore or chose not to wear on his uniform. Like Tucker the Major had American parachute wings on his shirt and, under those wings, were two rows of ribbons. The top row had a purple heart and a bronze star. The bottom row looked suspiciously like the campaign ribbons O'Connell's dad kept in a drawer in his home in Buffalo. The real puzzle was the leather jacket, which had a large American flag sewn on his left sleeve, but no aviator wings on the front. Instead, on the right sleeve a type of wings O'Connell had never seen before. They looked like British paratrooper wings but in the center were two red initials: SF.

O'Connell stood at attention and rendered a hand salute. Tucker returned the salute and started without preamble. Ruben Tucker was never one for pleasantries. "O'Connell, I want to ask you something."

"Sir."

"Do you like running your company?"

"Yes, sir. I am proud of my company."

"Do you want to leave this Regiment?"

"Sir, I do not want to leave this Regiment. I am a paratrooper and I intend to stay a paratrooper until a Nazi kills me or the war is over."

Tucker looked over at the officer to his left. "Bill, I think that says it all."

"Sir, with your permission, I need to ask the captain a question." Tucker nodded.

"Captain, are you willing to volunteer for additional and dangerous duty?"

O'Connell couldn't sort out where these questions were going. How much more dangerous could Army duty be than jumping out of airplanes, in the dark, behind enemy lines? "Sir, I am a paratrooper and I am always ready to take on additional duties and as a paratrooper I always assume they will be dangerous." It wasn't a perfect response. If fact as he said it, he realized it sounded plenty corny, but it was the best he could do under the circumstances. The priests and nuns in Catholic school and Canisius College had not taught him how to answer these types of questions. O'Connell figured the question must be about some new mission that the 504th had just received from the major. Perhaps Tucker wanted to determine if O'Connell and his company could do the job.

Tucker looked at the major. "That, Bill, was a trick question. However, I will accept the fact that you have outwitted me on this one and you have your man."

"Sir, it was not a trick question, it is the same question we always want to ask. The only difference is you let me ask it."

"Major, get out of here. O'Connell, you just volunteered to work for the major and his bunch of cut throats. I will have your orders cut today. Go back to your company, tell your XO to report to your battalion commander immediately and your first sergeant to report to the sergeant major at 1400hrs this afternoon. Dismissed." O'Connell rendered a salute, did an about face and left the tent. The major pulled on his coat and caught up with O'Connell as he headed back to his company tent.

O'Connell looked down at the major's boots and noticed they were very well-worn jump boots. This guy wasn't a garrison officer. He had done some fighting somewhere. The major said, "O'Connell, in case you didn't realize it, you just joined the OSS. I will be leaving on the next flight back to the States and you will be leaving with me. Pack your kit and get to the airfield by 1600hrs."

"Sir, I don't have a clue what the OSS is or why you think you need me or why I have just left the 504th."

"That, young O'Connell, is what you are about to learn."

>>>>>> RESISTANCE

December 1942 - October 1943 — Berlin, Rio de Janeiro,

Brazil and Panjim, Portuguese colony of Goa

A fter the failed operation in Palestine, Steinmark was evacuated from North Africa. A one-eyed commando was not going to be very successful in the field. As he recuperated, first in Vienna and eventually back in his home in Potsdam, he worried he would never return to the war. He found no appeal to living in Potsdam on a service pension while allied bombers pounded his country day and night. Even worse would be to work in some staff position among relics from the Great War and their supervisors who were all Nazi party members. Those Nazi posers worked especially hard to stay away from combat but wore beautifully tailored uniforms and rows of ribbons for service outside the war-zones of Russia and North Africa. As Steinmark sat in the family living room in Potsdam and walked each day to his doctor's appointment, he considered his options. None were good, but if he didn't do something, it was going to be service in Berlin. That simply would not do.

Both his parents had died in a car accident in 1936 on the newly created autobahn, so they never experienced anything but the successes of the Nazi party. He was certain that wartime Berlin was not what they would have expected. His only other relatives was his sister who was married to an engineer working on some sort of engineering project in Peenemunde, far from Potsdam. Steinmark had no reason to stay home and every intention of returning to the war. He couldn't say why he missed combat's mix of boredom and terror. Perhaps it was the comradeship, the rush of adrenaline before combat, or the incredible relief after a successful mission. The pain associated with his wound increased his desire to return to the war and do something, anything, to avenge his colleague lost in Palestine.

In December 1942, Steinmark used his status as a wounded war veteran from the Brandenburg Division to get an appointment with the head of the Abwehr, Admiral Canaris. He arrived in dress uniform wearing his recently issued Knight's Cross with Oak Leaves and with his combat service ribbons from the Eastern Front and Africa. He decided to wear an eye patch instead of his hospital issued glass eye to make sure Canaris would know immediately that he had made a sacrifice for the Fatherland. It surprised Steinmark that Canaris was ready with an offer for service in another part of the military intelligence world: an offer that would get him out of Berlin, out of Germany, and back into the war. After additional training, he would be serving as an intelligence officer under cover for the Abwehr, building sabotage networks against the British. It was not as good as serving as a Brandenburger on the front, but at least it was a real assignment.

It was a mission on the other side of the world in Goa, the Portuguese colony on the Indian Subcontinent. The service had established a reasonable cover for him. First, he would travel by submarine to South America. There he would link up with a network from the Abwehr and establish himself as a Brazilian trader, importing and exporting goods between the Portuguese colony and the South American nation. This fit well enough with his experiences between the wars working in South America and his Portuguese and Spanish language skills. The Abwehr already had a trading company in place in Goa, MERCURY CORPORACAO, which would suit the mission. Once established in the company, he traveled by steamer from Brazil to Portugal and from Portugal to Goa in June of 1943. Steinmark thought it amusing that his voyage from Brazil to Portugal included ship convoy protected from German U-boats by U.S. Navy destroyers. In the hold of the steamer, his trunks included one filled with his communications equipment, multiple currencies, and a small bag of diamonds. Further shipments of currency and, eventually, gold in British coins were promised once he was established in Goa as the new Brazilian representative for MERCURY CORPORACAO.

His real assignment was to find Indian resistance to the British Raj in Western India and use them to infiltrate the Royal Navy harbor in Bombay to sabotage Royal Navy ships. Train them, arm them, and let them loose in Western India: disrupt any ships sending Indian Army troops and supplies to Europe. He had authority from Admiral Canaris himself to expand the project in any way he could and, within reason, at whatever cost. Steinmark could use his training in German special operations to accomplish this task. It was a good mission for a one-eyed German commando.

By the fall of 1943, Steinmark, as Dom Maximilian Traumann, was fully engaged with Goa. He established himself as a South American playboy with money to spend and friends to make. He attended parties, bought two horses, stabled them in the best stables in town, and identified early on where the local elite ate, where they went for music and dancing and where they gambled. Dom Maximilian wore the right clothes, hosted the best parties for the right people and worked hard to make himself the very best of friends to the Portuguese Colonial Leadership. When MERCURY CORPORACAO ships under a Brazilian flag entered the harbor, the harbor master and customs officials, who were Steinmark's gambling partners, made sure the vessels docked on time and were handled quickly without the normal customs routine. In exchange, the Brazilian "trader" saw that these best of friends were compensated, either financially or with special gifts from South America.

As Major Jan Steinmark, the Abwehr agent, he built a network of safe sites from Goa to Bombay that would allow safe infiltration and exfiltration. He raised a team from the large smuggling clans that lived in the Portuguese Colony and traded up and down the Indian Coast. Steinmark was certain that before the war, most of these smugglers were coastal pirates looting unsuspecting cargo ships traveling along the Malabar Coast to and from Bombay. The war and the Royal Navy made smuggling far more lucrative and far less dangerous, so they easily transitioned into that profession. Steinmark simply expanded their financial opportunities. He paid in currency and diamonds and, eventually, British gold coins. He asked few questions and all he wanted was for them to obey tasking without question.

Of course there were some who tried to take advantage of his simple plan. Well before he formalized the smuggling network, he established a network of informants to report on the smugglers. He also hired a few local criminals to serve as enforcers. Their first job was to bring before Steinmark a smuggler suspected on cheating him. After a few broken fingers, the smuggler confessed his sins. Word soon got out along the docks and in the Goan and Indian underworld that it was dangerous to cross him. After the first "correction," Steinmark left it to his enforcers to ensure compliance with his requirements. No more broken bones were needed.

Once he was certain that his network was secure, Dom Maximilian left Goa on his small sailboat for a few days of fishing every month and Major Steinmark transitioned to his smuggler network, to travel the route to Bombay on his own. At his last safe house south of the fishing village of Kolaba near Bombay harbor, he sent out word that he was interested in listening to Indians who might oppose the British government in India. Those he met were dreamers or individuals committed to non-violent resistance. The Abwehr had provided details of how the Indian National Army supported the Japanese in Bengal and they expected him to create a similar force in Western India. He learned quickly that his area lacked raw material for such a force. He would have to find another way.

After "volunteering," O'Connell was sent stateside to attend multiple OSS training schools in the Washington DC Area. After he reported to an undercover training camp, he was told that the training would take four to six months, depending on his skills. Some of the training was based on the rigorous British commando school in Scotland and some mirrored the British Special Operations Executive training that took place at a facility in Ontario, Canada known as Special Training Site 103 or more commonly known to the OSS trainers and trainees as Camp X. The SOE had been in business since 1940, so they offered the most experience available for the new OSS mission.

As an Army officer, Peter O'Connell had been accustomed to following a strict chain of command. He quickly found that the Office of Strategic Services, or OSS, placed much more decision-making authority on individual officers. After nearly five months of training and briefings, O'Connell was barely coming to terms with this very different way of doing business. In the 504th, an officer's job was to turn specific orders into action. Here, there were seldom orders. In the OSS, you received directions such as "conduct espionage operations" or "engage in subversion and sabotage." You were expected to translate those directions into a plan of action and then conduct that action on your own or with members of a foreign resistance group who, you were warned, might or might not want your help.

His instructors regularly stated that everything behind enemy lines was unclear and dangerous. Following orders would get you killed. The OSS relied on their agents to turn directions into successful operations in whatever way they saw fit and in whatever way would keep them and their resistance partners alive. O'Connell admitted he liked the responsibility to make his own plans. That didn't make it any less confusing when his instructors answered every question with "Well, that depends."

Most of the training O'Connell attended was in the Catoctin Mountains of Maryland at a location the instructors called "The Farm" but officially known as Area B. The trainers were former police officers, British commandos, and some early OSS survivors of what they called "the field" meaning life behind enemy lines. The training was intense, exhausting and sometimes even brutal. They were taught how to use weapons, explosives, knives and even their bare hands to kill the enemy. He learned to use and maintain a variety of foreign weapons which were likely to be the stock-in-trade of his resistance fighters. Each lesson had to be repeated until it was second nature.

Unlike the training he received in the Army and with the 82nd, the instructors made it clear that while audacity was good, it was good only if it was blended with a large amount of caution. They taught that balancing risk versus gain was the most important point. The instructors stated this point at the beginning and end of the training: if you were uncovered, you would be hunted by a relentless and vicious security service. They told the recruits that Hitler had issued orders to kill all allied troops conducting operations behind enemy lines. There would be no quarter given, no prisoners taken. If on the odd chance that an OSS officer was captured, the prisoner could expect days of torture followed by a firing squad. In short, it was kill or be killed. More importantly, it was conduct the operation and evade capture so that you can live to fight another day.

O'Connell learned to communicate using a radio to send an enciphered Morse code message. This was considered an essential skill so that an OSS agent behind enemy lines could communicate with OSS headquarters to send reports, receive directions, and request resupply. He used a suitcase radio which was nothing more than a shortwave transmitter, a wire aerial and a morse code key that fit into a leather overnight case. They were also taught to set up and take down their radios quickly so that they never transmitted or received from the same place twice. German radio intercept and direction finding vehicles were everywhere and long transmissions or, worse still, multiple transmissions would enable the German Security Police, the GESTAPO, or the Nazi Security Service, the *Sicherheitsdienst* or SD, to fix the location and raid it immediately.

Just when the message "you are all alone and any mistake will kill you" began to capture his attention, O'Connell started the block of instruction on basic techniques for working with resistance fighters. His instructors pointed out that his single most important job was to enhance resistance operations in the field. He was no longer going to be a fighter, he was going to be advising fighters. O'Connell's greatest difficulty in the practical exercises that followed was learning to avoid giving orders. He needed to frame directions as suggestions. The instructors quoted numerous case studies from fifty years of irregular warfare but they came back to the simple statements provided in T.E. Lawrence's writings. Lawrence's work with the Arabs in World War I emphasized it was always better to let the locals do the work at whatever level they were capable than trying to force the locals to operate to some conventional military standard.

The final OSS training problem sent O'Connell to the New York City harbor with the mission to break into the Navy Yard and place dummy explosives in a cargo container about to be loaded on a Navy ship. His instructors told him, "O'Connell, you have to take a train from Baltimore to New York. We have told the Army counterintelligence folks there is a Nazi saboteur on the train posing as an Army captain. We have also told the Navy Shore Patrol personnel at the New York Navy Yard there is a threat of a saboteur trying to get into the Yard. They were not told this was a training exercise. The best you can hope for if you are caught is you spend days in jail before we get you out. The worst you can expect is they may shoot first and ask questions later. You have a week to travel there and do the job. Get to work!"

This was like no other exercise O'Connell had endured as a paratrooper or in the OSS. He was determined to put his training to the test. He avoided suspicion on the train by sitting with a group of Army and Navy recruits on their last leave before deployment. They spent their time from Baltimore to New York playing poker, sharing drinks from a paper sack and generally blowing off steam. Once in New York, O'Connell spent three nights watching the docks from a coffee shop window. Once he knew how the docks worked, what dock-workers looked like and the timing of the security patrols, O'Connell was ready to do his job. He went to a local Salvation Army outpost favored by the seamen looking for a free meal and a free bed between jobs. One night while in the Salvation Army, he borrowed a peacoat and dock ID from one of the sailors sleeping off a long night at a bar. With this light disguise, O'Connell slipped onto the docks. Then he used his lock picking skills to enter one of the supply warehouses and place the dummy explosives in a real crate of supplies to be loaded the next day on a ship headed to England.

The same evening, he returned the coat and ID, called his OSS training contact in New York from a phone booth near the docks to report accomplishing the mission and went to the OSS safehouse to shave, wash up and change into another set of clothes waiting for him. His success was an embarrassment to both the Army and Navy security forces and another opportunity for General Donovan to note the skills of his program to the President and the Joint Chiefs.

Before deploying back to the war, O'Connell received a brief furlough at home in Buffalo, where he learned it was his father who had "recruited" him into the OSS. For the first time in his life, he learned about his father's time in the trenches and his links to General Donovan. His father had kept all of the ugly side of war from him until this trip. Now Peter could understand why his father never talked about his war and why he would have trouble talking about this war, his war. Whether that was a good thing or a bad thing, he couldn't say. It was clear that his father was pleased to see he was working for General Donovan and his mother was just pleased to see her son after two years. They decided to make a Thanksgiving dinner on Halloween and O'Connell enjoyed giving out candies to the local kids walking down the streets of south Buffalo. There was rationing and plenty of houses with blue stars and a few gold stars in the windows, but otherwise, it was easy to forget for a moment that there was a war going on.

Once the furlough was over, O'Connell received orders to travel to the OSS office in Cairo. He arrive in Cairo tired, dirty and smelling of aviation fuel from riding in cargo planes, seaplanes and bombers. The OSS team quickly put him to work. After a three week crash course in Italian, he learned he was going to link up with Navy Commander James Sciandretti who was running a resistance circuit, code named VIGNETTE. Sciandretti was in the Apennine Mountains working with the Italian resistance made up of rural partisans who hated the Fascists and lived with family vendettas that were centuries old. The only way to get to Sciandretti was by a night parachute drop.

On 01 December, Cairo sent O'Connell to Palestine to attend a jump school run by the British SOE. At first, O'Connell insisted that as a US paratrooper, he didn't need additional parachute training. That argument didn't hold any water at the SOE school. On arrival at jump school, the SOE trainers, all senior British sergeants used to recalcitrant officers and terrified civilian agents, explained to O'Connell that he wasn't going to be jumping out of a Dakota like US and UK paratroopers. Instead, he was going to be jumping through "a Joe Hole" which they chose not to explain to this newly arrived student. Also, they told O'Connell he wouldn't get a reserve parachute. "Too low to make any difference" the senior instructor said with smile. Finally, he wasn't going to be carrying his Garand rifle in a canvas bag at his side but carrying a M1 carbine or a Thompson submachine gun strapped across his chest where a reserve parachute was normally located. A few more descriptions of the ways of the SOE jump school, including the demonstration of his jump-suit coveralls and his parachute helmet that looked, more or less, like a leather football helmet, and O'Connell agreed, he didn't know much about special operations parachuting. He was relieved they didn't make him attend the standard ground school, but he did make five parachute jumps to be certified for OSS parachute operations.

O'Connell's training jumps included three from a tethered balloon and two from an old Halifax bomber. O'Connell finally learned the definition of a "Joe Hole." The "Joe Hole" was called that because for security purposes the aircraft crew were never told the real name of their jumpers, so all their jumpers were referred to as "Joe." It was called a hole because it was just that, a hole cut in the bottom of the fuselage, in some cases where the bottom gun turret had been located. It took some getting used to even for an experienced jumper since instead of a jump, the paratrooper pushed off the leading edge of the hole and fell out the bottom of the aircraft.

As with his previous experience, O'Connell found the jumps terrifying and exhilarating. One thing that was better than jumps with the 504th was he was not expected to jump with 50 pounds of kit attached to his body. The hope was that most of the key material would follow him to the drop zone in parachute bundles dropped after the jumper. At the end of the training, the instructors issued O'Connell a new set of wings with an SF standing for Special Forces and a British paratrooper red beret with standard British jump wings attached. The instructors told O'Connell he could wear the SF wings on his chest until he made a combat jump. After that, they went on his right shoulder. They made it clear that this was right and proper and a protocol that should not be violated. O'Connell thanked the instructors and headed back to Cairo to wait for the flight taking him to meet Sciandretti and the Italian resistance members of VIGNETTE.

After two months of listening to dreamers, Steinmark had taken another route to accomplish his mission. Financial incentives would be far more useful than ideology. He used his smuggling network to identify leaders of criminal gangs operating in Bombay. The smugglers provided ten names and he invited two — Haji Din Mohammed and Arjuna Golpani — for a meeting to discuss "a lucrative opportunity." The reports on both men were favorable. Din Mohammed represented the Bombay extension of a bandit clan from the lower Indus River region of the Sindh. These bandits, known as dacoits, for generations had been intercepting cargo on the river and even attacking British rail carriages headed to Karachi. Din Mohammed was sent to Bombay to expand the family business. Arjuna Golpani started his "career" in Bombay as a street thug. His family were washermen, dhobis in Hindi, and he decided early on that regardless of caste restrictions, he wasn't going to be a dhobi. He built his own street gang in the slums near the commercial harbor and over the previous ten years had expanded his network to include extortion, murder for hire and robbery, especially robbery in the Muslim neighborhoods. Steinmark liked Din Mohammed because of the regional links and Arjuna Golpani simply for his audacity and cunning.

When the leaders agreed to the meeting, Steinmark left Goa on his sailboat, transitioned to the most impressive of his smuggler's boats, made all the more impressive now that they were armed with German light and heavy machine guns, and headed along the Malabar Coast. At a small cove surrounded by high cliffs, he sent a dinghy to bring the two men from the shore. Both had bodyguards who insisted on attending, but they were persuaded to stay on the beach when they saw the working end of the submachine guns carried by Steinmark's men.

Steinmark welcomed his newly arrived guests on his sailboat. He had tea for the Muslim and whiskey for the Hindu. He had a small lunch of Indian dumplings known as pakoras: meat filled for Din Mohammed and vegetable filled for Golpani.

Steinmark spoke in his most formal English. "Gentlemen, first I want to thank you for taking the time to see me. I have heard much of your exploits in Bombay. I hope I can add to your profits while you pursue my mission to undermine the British Navy."

Golpani nodded as he worked over the vegetable pakoras and Steinmark's whiskey. Golpani realized that both the food, the tray and the glasses were all polluted by this foreigner, but he was willing to listen if there was some profit to be made.

Steinmark noted Golpani's silence as well as Din Mohammed's drinking habits. Instead of the tea, Din Mohammed poured himself a large whiskey in one of Steinmark's crystal glasses and downed it in one swallow. As he poured himself another glass, the Muslim villain nearly cracking the whiskey glass when he bashed the crystal decanter against the rim. Golpani gazed at Din Mohammed with emotionless features. Steinmark remained silent.

After finishing the second glass, Din Mohammed said, "I came here with the understanding that we were going to negotiate a business arrangement. I had no idea that I would have to share my day with this polytheist miscreant."

Steinmark said, "Sir, I believe you are both more than capable of helping in this opportunity, but I think it will be safer for all of us if we have both of your networks working on the project. Please let me explain…"

Din Mohammed poured himself another healthy portion of whiskey. Steinmark noted that the man had yet to eat anything. While it was possible that this man had a strong resistance to drink, but Steinmark was beginning to worry about a man who seemed to have so little self-control. Of all traits Steinmark demanded of his new organization, self-control was the most important. Espionage and sabotage could survive audacity and even bad fortune, but it could not survive personal weaknesses.

Din Mohammed said, "I already know what you want from me. You want my people to work for you and your Nazi masters. I hate the British who think they are our masters, but I don't want to trade one master for another. So, unless there is real profit in this, I am not excited to help you." He waved toward Golpani and continued, "Perhaps this Hindi manager of a flea sized syndicate will serve you, but I suspect I will not."

Steinmark noted that Din Mohammed was beginning to show the effects of the whiskey. He had become more bellicose and was waving his hands. At one point, he lost grip on the crystal glass that held his fourth whiskey and the glass fell to the oak deck and shattered. Steinmark winced.

"Sir, I hope you will change your mind when I explain our offer to you. We simply want you to expand your established networks in the harbor, continue to apply pressure on the men who work on the dry docks and ship fitters. You will be paid handsomely to create slow downs at the port and to periodically *insist* in your own creative way that they conduct small scale sabotage at the docks. We will pay you in gold."

Golpani followed the conversation carefully and Steinmark noted Golpani nodded gently at each point that he made. The Hindu was definitely interested. As he was about to ask Golpani his thoughts, Din Mohammed intruded again after he grabbed Steinmark's own whiskey glass and downed the drink in one gulp. "You are wasting your time talking to this Hindu. I can do all of this. It is easy. It is too easy. I will do this, but you will pay me a good price and you will pay me in advance!"

With that exclamation, Din Mohammed leaned over, tipping over the table with the food, the glasses and the crystal decanter. He jabbed two fingers into Steinmark's chest to emphasize his point. Steinmark's crew, daggers drawn, started for Din Mohammed. Steinmark halted them with a wave of his right hand. Though already wooly headed from the whiskey, Din Mohammed had been watching Steinmark and his right hand as he approached the German. The wave distracted him just enough that he had ignored Steinmark's left hand reaching into a jacket pocket. When Steinmark lost his right eye, he spent months in rehabilitation learning to shoot with his left hand. All of his smugglers knew what would happen next. Out of his jacket pocket he pulled a small Mauser. One round from the Mauser entered just under Din Mohammed's jaw and excited the top of his head. The argument resolved, Steinmark's crew thought it was an excellent joke. They grabbed Din Mohammed and tossed the dying man over the side.

At that point, Steinmark turned to Golpani and said, "I apologize for my rude guest and my own actions. I hope this has not caused you great discomfort. I would very much like you to consider my offer to work on this project. Now, it would appear you would be my only representative in Bombay." As Steinmark spoke, his crew had moved directly behind Golpani. If the Hindu was equally reckless, they were prepared to respond.

For the first time since their initial greetings, Golpani spoke. "Sir, my discomfort is of no concern to you. I have lived with discomfort my whole life. I promise you that I will do the job and you will be happy."

Steinmark stood up and put his two hands together in the Hindu style of farewell and said, "Mr. Golpani, I am sure we will be happy in our new business arrangement." He then waved to the crew to take Golpani ashore. Long before they arrived at the beach, Golpani's men had killed Din Mohammed's bodyguards.

Within two weeks, Steinmark's intelligence network in Bombay reported a rise in sabotage, extortion and threats to family members of workers at the Bombay harbor. Golpani clearly understood he was being paid for performance and that pay came only after Steinmark had confirmed their claims. If, or more likely when, any of Golpani's men were caught, they would be identified as part of a criminal gang rather than a German special operation. It was low cost and low risk. Abwehr sources inside the British Naval Command in Bombay reported directly to Berlin that both the Royal Marine security personnel and the British Special Branch were experiencing significant damage at the port and had yet to determine the source. Meanwhile, Dom Maximilian Traumann spent pleasant evenings entertaining and being entertained by the elite of Goa as the Christmas holidays arrived.

Christmas Eve 24 December 1943 Cairo

and the Apennine Mountains of Italy

After waiting for an aircraft, the right weather and the right moonlight, the day finally came for O'Connell's insertion. OSS "dispatchers" took him to the airfield outside Cairo and linked him up with his plane. The US Army Air Force had a special unit for OSS missions. They called themselves "The Carpetbaggers" and flew B24 Liberator bombers painted matte black. The B24 had exceptional range and with modifications, it was the perfect platform for cargo and agent delivery. The cargo was dropped out of the bomb bay doors and the agents jumped from the "Joe Hole." Flights took place only during the two weeks of the best moonlight because the B24s flew at low altitude with the navigator working in the old bombardier position in the nose of the aircraft. From that position, he used ground features as much as his navigation skills to get the cargo and "Joes" to the right place at the right time. The Carpetbaggers flew alone, without fighter escort and only two gunners, in the top turret and the tail gunner position, to extend their range. Since all the missions were secret, the Carpetbaggers' courage and commitment to the mission was known only to their colleagues in the OSS.

On his delivery mission, O'Connell was the only "Joe" in the aircraft, but the crew had several supply drops to make before they delivered him and his cargo to the mountains north and east of Rome.

O'Connell periodically checked the radium dial on his Bulova watch, but time seemed to slow to a crawl as he waited for his turn in the cycle. It was a long, cold, and dark ride, but O'Connell was wearing his SOE jumpsuit over a newly issued wool trousers and a leather flight jacket with a large American Flag stitched on the sleeve. The hope was that if the aircraft went down or if he was captured early in his deployment, the flight jacket would allow him to claim he was a downed airman trying to evade capture. He was warm enough, but still pre-jump nerves prevented O'Connell from getting even a little nap over the two hours.

Eventually, the crew chief pulled open the hatch for the Joe Hole. Once the Joe Hole was open, it was all business. O'Connell moved from his sling seat on the skin of the aircraft to the floor. After attaching his static line to a steel cable running down the length of the aircraft, he pushed himself on the floor just forward of the hole. While O'Connell was moving into position, the crew chief ran his gloved hands along the edge of the opening to ensure there were no sharp edges that might slice the static line. He then walked behind O'Connell and double checked the end of the static line where it was attached to the aircraft and traced the line back to O'Connell's parachute pack. He walked in front of O'Connell and gave him a thumbs up. For the next few minutes, they both waited in the dark looking at a small set of lights rigged next to what was previously the waist gun position of the aircraft. When the red light illuminated, both the crew chief and the "Joe" knew they were one minute out from the drop zone and it was time for O'Connell to put his feet through the hatch. Green light on and O'Connell pushed off into the darkness.

O'Connell was used a brutal opening shock from his previous jumps. This OSS jump was no different though he carried less equipment. The design of the parachute created a "crack the whip" opening shock. As he looked up to check his canopy, he could see the supply bundles for his new unit leaving the bomb bay of the B24 and the parachutes opening. He looked up one last time at the aircraft and all he could see was the red-hot exhaust pipes from the bomber. Suddenly, the aircraft banked and disappeared into the night. The bundles and O'Connell landed inside a circle of burning barrel fires that marked the drop zone. By the time he was out of his parachute harness, the fires in the barrels were out and the bundles recovered.

Next was the introduction to the "reception committee" of Italian resistance fighters on the drop zone. O'Connell's paratroopers in the 504th might have been a group of criminals and roughnecks before the war, but they were disciplined soldiers by 1943. The Italian resistance fighters offered no promise of discipline. They were dressed in a mix of wool and leather, various types of headgear and all wore thick beards. Each of the partisans felt it was essential to welcome O'Connell with a bear hug and shout a greeting. He noticed after the first two hugs that the partisans were using the hug to check how many weapons he carried under the coverall. As far as O'Connell was concerned, the only good thing about this revelation was that they didn't try to steal any of his weapons.

After the greetings, the recently arrived parachute bundles were opened. The cargo was dispersed among the men and the parachutes and O'Connell's coverall were buried in the forest. O'Connell followed his hosts up a mountain trail for nearly three hours. O'Connell thought himself fit after paratrooper training and the advanced training he received from the OSS in the US, Cairo, and Palestine but he was exhausted when he finally arrived at base camp which was nothing more than a clearing in the woods with three green, canvas tarps strung between some of the trees.

Sitting in front of a small fire was another of the Italian bandits. Unshaven, dressed in a mix of leather, wool and rags. In the firelight, O'Connell finally noticed the leather flying jacket with a US flag stitched to the left sleeve and SF wings on his chest as well as a long faded green beret that O'Connell had seen British Commandos wear in Sicily. The man in the beret stood up and offered a barely clean hand. "Jim Sciandretti. I'm assuming you are Peter O'Connell."

"Yes, sir."

"Merry Christmas and welcome to Partisan country, O'Connell. Coffee?"

O'Connell shook his head. All he needed now was sleep.

Sciandretti sat back down and offered O'Connell another wooden crate to sit on. He took a sip from his porcelain mug and said, "Let me offer some rules of the road that you need to know before you crawl into your blanket here in our luxurious apartment." O'Connell knew Sciandretti was a Navy Commander, equivalent to an Army Lieutenant Colonel and the *VIGNETTE* team leader. He forced himself to wake up, at least a little and listen for more detailed instructions of the ground tactical situation like he would have received from his battalion commander in the 504th.

Instead, he got his first lesson in working with Partisans. "Peter, you are here to work with one of the Italian teams we support in the mountains. When I arrived here courtesy of a US Navy submarine, I was certain my job was to command the Partisans and defeat the Germans in our area. I'm a Navy officer after all and Navy officer training emphasized command. That is, designing a plan and making sure your subordinates execute the plan." O'Connell wasn't entirely certain where this was going and he already wished he had taken the offer of coffee.

Sciandretti looked at O'Connell's falling eyelids, reached over to the coffee pot and poured a second cup. He handed the cup to O'Connell and shouted "Wake up!" O'Connell startled at Sciandretti's shout, almost fell off the crate he was on. He realized he had been asleep and couldn't remember what Sciandretti had said. He took the offered cup and started to drink.

"As I was saying before you fell asleep, the United States Navy expects its officers to command. When I joined the OSS right after it started in June of '42, they sent me to train in Canada at Camp X. Our training was mostly on how to stay alive behind the lines and how to conduct sabotage operations using SOE equipment. Next stop was to British commando school and SOE airborne school in the UK and then by submarine to the Italian coast. James Sciandretti had arrived to take command! Well, I learned pretty damn quick that I was wrong." Sciandretti stopped and watched O'Connell drink some coffee.

It gave Sciandretti time to think about his first days in Italy and tell O'Connell a story. Sciandretti said, "The British Navy sailors rowed the rubber boat toward the shore of Mussolini's Italy. I was in the center of the boat with my sea bag, my Thompson submachine gun at the ready. According to instructions in Gibraltar, SOE team *Harriet* with one of their Partisan teams would meet me and the rest would be up to me." Sciandretti paused to take a drink from his coffee cup and determine if any of this was reaching his new partner.

"I could see the flashlight signal on the beach as the sailors paddled to the shore. Friend or foe? It would be the first of many times I had to trust my SOE colleagues and hope for the best. The Italian partisans who met me were thrilled to see an American coming to help. Several of the partisans had worked in New York or Boston on the docks in the 1930s and their greeting showed it. If I had expected a clandestine welcome I was mistaken. From the shoreline, I heard voices shouting, "Welcome America! We love the Yankees!" Another voice, louder this time said, "NO, WE LOVE THE RED SOX!" So much for a quiet entrance into theatre.

Over the next few days and once the SOE contacts turned me over to my own set of Partisans, the Italians made it abundantly clear they were not interested in my bright ideas on how to make their operations better. Instead, they spent time showing me how they did their job and what they needed. What they needed were supplies. What they didn't need from me was advice even if I could speak Italian and my grandparents and my father were from Naples. I learned his first lesson of Partisan Warfare: The guerrillas already knew how to fight and how to stay alive as hunted men. What they needed were guns, ammunition and explosives. The sooner I could deliver them, the better they could do their job in their way and the happier they would be with young Lieutenant Commander Sciandretti." Another cup of coffee and a check to see if O'Connell was following any of this. It appeared he was on his way to dreamland, so Sciandretti offered one last thought.

"The second lesson I learned was there is no single resistance in here. Instead, there are many Partisan groups who do not work together because they represent different factions with vendettas that could be traced back before there even was an Italy. I found that out the hard way on my first linkup with SOE team *Harriet* and their Partisans. While I was talking to my British colleagues about coordinating future operations, a knife fight broke out between my guides and the guides from the SOE commander. Hours later, when we were back at their base camp, I asked one of the Partisans, what caused the fight.

The partisan I asked said, "We hate them, Jimmy. We hate them with all our heart. Well, not as much as we hate the Fascisti, but longer, harder hate. We have been fighting them for years. When this war is over and the Fascisti are gone, we will be fighting them again. Tonight, it was just a reminder to them that this is only a truce, not a surrender."

Through his sleepy haze, O'Connell heard Sciandretti say, "And that is why you need to listen more than you need to speak." Sciandretti stopped to take a sip from his mug. "I hear you speak some Italian and that's swell. Don't press your luck. I thought I was fluent when I got here and my opinion of my Italian changed pretty damn quick. A number of the Partisans worked on the docks in the US before the war. Their English is better than your Italian or mine," Sciandretti paused. "Use them as your interpreters and limit your language to greetings and simple requests. Also, don't joke around with these guys in Italian or in English. You don't know their version of humor and they won't have any trouble killing you on a point of honor if you irritate them." Another pause, another sip of coffee. "Remember, this is their fight. They may need guidance and they definitely need supplies, but they are not going to take instruction. Help them, but don't expect to lead them." Sciandretti looked him in the eye and finished by saying, "Now, go back to sleep. I hope you heard a little of the story and, maybe, even learned a lesson tonight. Tomorrow you have to get on the trail with your new team of Partisans. We need to finish off constructing a larger drop zone for the next resupply. And, by the way, when I say we, I really mean you. I may not be here tomorrow when you wake up from your beauty sleep, I have an ambush I have to set up with another set of these bandits. Oh, and if you can kill some Germans or Italian Fascists along the way to the drop zone, so much the better. Good night."

O'Connell woke at dawn after three hours of restless sleep on a bed of pine needles and dirt. He struggled to get out of his sleeping bag and move from flat on his back, to sitting up and eventually to standing up. He wasn't certain if it was the jump, the hike or the bed that made every joint ache. Looking down at him was the third member of the OSS party for *VIGNETTE*. Like Sciandretti, his clothes could not be described as anything resembling a uniform. He was wearing an Army field jacket with the flag on one sleeve and the OSS wings on the other. His non-uniform uniform was topped by what looked like some sort of green wool hunting cap with earflaps. He had a smirk on his face and two cups of steaming coffee in his hands. "Peter, if you would like some fresh coffee for your Christmas Breakfast, here's your cup. Don't worry about the aches and pains of sleeping in the rough. No Army cots out here. Anyhow, you aren't going to get much sleep."

"Thanks for the coffee and the warning. Who the heck are you?"

"Tech Sergeant Tim Loftis. Communicator, logistics specialist, periodic herder of sheep and goats, and a pretty good demo man if you ever need one."

"Thanks, Tim. Will we be working together?"

"You must be kidding. I rarely see Jim and I doubt I will see you much. I have to move the base camp every so often so the Nazis can't use their RDF trucks to find us. You go out and do what you do, I will be back here doing what I do. Still, when you get back to camp, there will always be coffee."

As Loftis paused to drink his coffee, O'Connell heard something between a growl and a shout. Clearly Sciandretti was still in camp and shouting, "OK, so you have had your nap, your coffee and your introductions, let's get to work." He was surrounded by a number of the Resistance fighters and looking at a map spread out on the dirt. Two Partisans were sitting cross legged on the ground. O'Connell grabbed the coffee from Loftis and spilled half the cup as he ran over to the meeting.

Loftis shook his head, finished his cup and headed back to the stove and his radio rig. He figured it was up to the new guy to sort things out for himself. He was just surprised that Sciandretti hadn't told the new guy last night that he was replacing a guy who was killed because he got between two Partisans fighting over a local Italian maid. Probably best not to talk about that. But still, it could have served as a useful warning to stay clear of Italian women.

After a brief introduction and instructions on where Sciandretti wanted his new drop zone constructed, Sciandretti headed in one direction and O'Connell headed in another with his new resistance translator and guide, Carlo Guido. Guido had worked on the docks in Boston in the 1920s and early 1930s and spoke Boston accented English. O'Connell had always attributed a Boston accent to the wealthy of the Northeast so there were mental gymnastics required to listen to a partisan who looked like a bandit but spoke perfect Bostonian English. As they walked toward his new team and toward the new drop zone, Guido talked. A lot.

"So, boss. You're a paratrooper, right? I heard from one of my cousins in the US that they are as tough as Marines. You think so? My family says my cousin is a Marine in the Pacific. They wanted him to join the Marines so he wouldn't have to come to Europe and kill

Italians. You see we have plenty of Fascisti in our family, so they were probably right." He paused only long enough to take a breath before he started in again. O'Connell was more than happy that Guido was a talker because they were climbing up a ridge line that had O'Connell unable to say anything.

"You are an officer, huh? So, some fancy school and big deal family back home right? You are an American nobleman." Guido looked at him and it was clear that like it or not, O'Connell was going to have to answer. He stopped for a moment to catch his breath.

O'Connell laughed. "Nope. My dad is a railroad engineer. I got a scholarship out of Catholic school to a Catholic University in my home town. Joined the Army. I'll find work when I get home."

"Railroad? My cousin Vinnie is a steam engine mechanic for the Lackawanna Railroad. You know it?"

"Big Railroad all up and down the East Coast. My dad is with the New York Central."

"Well, if you are from a railroad family, then you can't be all bad. Your dad in a union?"

O'Connell wasn't clear where this was going, but answered truthfully, "Yes, I think it's called the Brotherhood of Locomotive Firemen and Engineers."

"How about you?"

"No unions in the United States Army, Carlo."

"Too bad. We like unions here. We are communists so we like unions."

O'Connell was puzzled and wasn't quite sure where the conversation was meant to go. His understanding of communism wasn't much more than the epithet used by his priests in Catholic school: "the godless communists." He wasn't sure how to have a political conversation with his partisan colleague, so all he could only think of a simple query, "Why?"

"My cousin Michael, he went to Spain to fight the Fascists. I don't know why he did that, but he did. He came home and told us only the communists were fighting the Fascists. So, when we decided to fight the Fascists here, he said we were now Communists. All the unions joined the resistance. Maybe not all fighting, but all doing something against the Fascists and the Nazis. See?" With that comment, Guido took off at an even more brutal pace as they headed to where the team was waiting.

S teinmark sat in his apartment overlooking the harbor. He had just finished sending the latest report to Berlin on his efforts targeting the British Navy Yards in Bombay.

Steinmark was pleased and he expected his annual report would be well received by Berlin. Now it was time to get ready for the evening. He had to bathe and change into his best formal clothes. He would attend a number of New Year's holiday events tonight. He spent New Year's Eve at the residence of the Portuguese Governor General chatting with senior members of the business community and watching the fireworks in the harbor. After years of combat operations, Steinmark had lost his interest in fireworks. The noise and the smell of gunpowder took him back to the Eastern Front where none of the memories were pleasant. In the Portuguese community, surrounded by members of neutral countries who had never seen war, Steinmark was careful not to reveal the tension that the fireworks created.

One thing that did help was the charming company of a young woman. She was the daughter of an Irish commercial trader in Dublin who was sent to Goa to keep up a steady trade between the Irish Free State and the Portuguese Her company and the Portuguese sparkling wines had made the evening tolerable. In today's report to Berlin, he asked for additional information on this woman. Steinmark knew that the Abwehr had a substantial network in the Irish Free State. They should be able to provide some background on a woman who claimed to be running a distant outpost for an Irish company. Along with being enjoyable company, Steinmark thought she might be an interesting tool to use in his operations in Bombay.

Unfortunately, tonight he did not expect to enjoy her company. Tonight would end with a night of cards with the chief of the local police, the mayor of Panjim and the Portuguese harbor master. Not difficult work, but he needed to use the evening to identify possible targets for recruitment and to convince the local authorities to look the other way with his efforts at the port. Steinmark finished burning the one-time pad cipher he had just used to send the latest message. Once completed, he headed for his bathroom. The memory of Judith Connelly was still there. He needed to find a way to spend more time with the red-haired girl. She might be nearly twenty years younger, but she seemed interested and her company would help with the lonely nights. She might be simply a diversion or she might become a new part of his network. In the espionage trade, there were always opportunities and anything seemed possible at the beginning of 1944.

In his first weeks in the mountains, O'Connell learned that his group of Italian partisans had been bandits and smugglers before the war and were still bandits and smugglers despite the war. Their view on "resistance" was simple. Kill as many Germans and Italian Fascists as they could until the war was over. Ideally, kill Germans and Fascists in truck convoys filled with supplies. These supplies were divided up evenly among the team after all their enemies were killed.

"See. We are communists," Guido said. "Everyone gets a share." Unfortunately, the division of the spoils often kept the team on the ambush site far longer than O'Connell liked. But, he realized leaving perfectly good cargo, no matter what the cargo was, just didn't make any sense to his Italian fighters. What didn't make good sense to O'Connell was the team's determination to deliver the spoils to their extended family members living in the mountains. These weren't places to cache weapons for the future, they were gifts to the family to demonstrate their skills as fighters.

O'Connell's team seemed to be made up entirely of the extended Guido family. The team leader was Carlo's cousin. The two sections in the team were led by Carlo's brothers. His cousins and second cousins and uncles made up most of the two dozen fighters. At one point, O'Connell told Carlo, "Just identify the guys who aren't your family and I'll assume everyone else is a relative."

Carlo Guido started to laugh and immediately translated O'Connell's "joke" to the entire team. The entire team shouted "Bravo, American!" and that was the beginning of O'Connell's education as an OSS agent with the Italian resistance. In discussions with his fighters both before and after ambushes, O'Connell came to realize that after the war, they all intended to get back to their normal village life including family feuds and defeating any government effort to control their lucrative legal and illegal businesses in the mountains. Family feuds might just include vendettas against locals who had tolerated the Fascisti or were relatives of the Fascisti. O'Connell eventually decided that whether the team were communists, criminals, smugglers, or just villagers, it wasn't going to be his business. Right now, they were all on the same side and that was good enough since they were good at killing Germans.

Just when O'Connell would be ready to give up on their lack of discipline, he would see evidence at least his small part of the Italian resistance was filled with descendants of the Roman centurions. Each partisan wanted to prove he had more endurance and was more courageous than the others. It became clear after the first ambush that O'Connell's greatest challenge was to organize that desire into effective sabotage operations where stealth was more important than audacity. Still, when it came to ambushes and raids, the partisans excelled. Over time, the team did accept some additional firearms training from O'Connell which made them to be even better killers. After one training session and a subsequent ambush where their new found skills allowed for a more effective kill zone with less risk, once again they cheered "Bravo, American!"

30 January 1944, Emilia-Romagna, Apennine Mountains,
Italian Partisan country

O'Connell walked toward a small mountain hut that now served as their field headquarters. The hut was really nothing more than a wooden extension out of a cave in the mountain rocks. The smell of a small wood-burning stove mixed with damp air reminded him of the Northern Pennsylvania hunting camps where his father took him during deer hunting season. The primary difference with that memory - other than the distance between Pennsylvania and Central Italy - was that O'Connell and the other two men of OSS team *VIGNETTE* were the hunted not the hunters. As the instructors had warned at the Farm, the Germans were relentless and once they realized they had a resistance team in their area, they spent days hunting them. For three weeks, the teams had harassed the Germans through raids and ambushes. Now, German army units were entering the small villages along the river valleys feeding into the Tiber in hopes of catching the Partisans and their OSS partners outright or identifying base camps through their radio direction finding equipment. Once the camps were located, they would be attacked by Stuka bombers. So far, his team of fighters had stayed one step ahead of the Germans as they conducted multiple raids and ambushes.

Today was the first time he had seen Jim Sciandretti in ten days, and he was looking forward to some company with a fellow American and a bit of rest without fear. Sciandretti was sitting on a three-legged, wooden milking stool in front of an upturned wooden crate that served as his field desk. Sometime in the past the crate had carried canned goods being shipped by truck to an Italian village called Tivoli. The label was partially scraped off, but it looked to O'Connell like the original shipment was for canned tomatoes. Sciandretti had several days beard, his hair was plastered to his head from the dampness and from the green beret planted on the back of his head. He looked like he hadn't slept in days.

Sciandretti was wearing the same clothes that O'Connell saw him in when he left ten days ago and the same clothes he was wearing when O'Connell arrived a month ago. It was his "uniform" but would never be described as Army regulation. The only items that were not in tatters or repaired using thread stitches like Frankenstein's monster were his leather flying jacket and his German mountaineering boots. The jacket was lined with sheepskin and it looked like it had seen more than one hard landing, most likely by parachute. After his first meeting with Sciandretti, O'Connell had wondered about the boots. Until this moment, there hadn't been any time to ponder it further as he had been on the run with his Partisan unit.

"O'Connell give me some good news today. I've had enough crap for now. I just received word from headquarters that the Army outside Monte Casino doesn't think we are working fast enough to attack the Germans. Luckily, I had to take down the transmitter before I could order Loftis to send something rude." Sciandretti pulled the stained and faded beret off his head and tossed it on the crate. He took a drink of coffee from a steaming porcelain cup that was balanced on the crate next to his notebook, a local map, his unholstered .45 pistol and now his beret.

O'Connell hadn't quite figured out yet what good news really looked like. They had been hunted by Germans behind the lines for the last ten days and it rained, snowed or sleeted every day since he arrived a month ago. Not much "good" about that. The fact that his team survived and he was now speaking without the use of a translator to another American seemed like good news…at least to O'Connell.

He said, "Boss, we conducted three ambushes over the last ten days on German convoys along the Tiber. A dozen trucks destroyed, probably fifty Germans and the same number of Fascists killed. The guys were pleased because the trucks were filled with German supplies including a couple of German anti-tank guns. Also, we just about completed clearing the drop zone for tomorrow's resupply. The guys are pretty motivated since I told them winter boots were arriving along with rifles, ammunition and more explosives."

Sciandretti looked up at O'Connell when he mentioned the resupply drop, "That's just swell, O'Connell, but I didn't order boots."

"I did back in November just before I left Cairo and I jumped into this garden spot. I looked at the terrain and thought about the weather. I tried to decide if field jackets or boots were the best choice for the bundles. I decided boots. We can get more boots in a bundle than field jackets. Whether we are getting them on this drop is any man's guess."

"O'Connell, I like the way you think, but you need to know the partisans have no sense of humor when it comes to resupply. You don't promise anything on resupply unless you *know* the item is certain to arrive. There better be some boots in one of the bundles the Carpetbaggers drop, or you and Loftis are giving up your boots tomorrow night," Sciandretti paused and continued, "I barely kept my head attached to my shoulders the first drop I managed. The drop did not include enough weapons for everyone in the Partisan unit and it didn't have any boots. They were convinced that it was a capitalist plot. The communist political commissar for the cell told them it was my fault."

"Shit, boss. What did you do?"

"First, I gave up my boots to the local leader. Then, I told them that their commie boss had requested a separate drop of supplies in the next valley so he could control who got what. I told them that given my loyalty to their cause," Sciandretti rolled his eyes, "I complied with his request. I told them to go visit him in his villa and ask him where he kept his portion of the weapons."

"And?"

"I think he made his escape before they killed him and dumped him in the Tiber, but I don't know for sure. Hell, it was his own fault convincing the guys that there was some sort of chicanery. Anyhow, once he was gone, things got better for us, so it was a win. The resistance folks found a pair of German boots for me and it was all good."

O'Connell thought about the skill it would take to spin a tale that both saved his life and pointed the finger at someone else. He doubted he could do it. "Boss, my guys say they are communists. Is that a problem?"

"Eh? What do you mean they are communists?"

"They don't really have any sort of political opinions. They just assume that everyone in the resistance are communists because only communists are in the resistance. My priests in Catholic school wouldn't like that logic, but that's what they said."

"And has that made any difference in their job of killing Nazis?"

"Nope."

"Then for now, O'Connell, I wouldn't spend a lot of time worrying about it. We aren't here to sort out future Italian politics. We are here to kill Nazis. As I said previously, if some communist political commissar gets in the way, then you have to worry."

"Boss, given what I've seen of the Guido family, I suspect a political commissar wouldn't last more than an hour before they dropped him in some abandoned well. These guys aren't interested in any sort of party discipline."

Sciandretti nodded and said, "Exactly."

O'Connell changed the subject, "Boss, what are we going to do with the explosives once we get them secured?"

"You mean other than annoy the crap out of the Germans?"

"Well, I was hoping for more strategic guidance than that."

"OK, if you insist on knowing everything, I guess I'll have to tell you. After all, you are my deputy."

"Boss, there are only three of us: you, me and Tim."

"And, I outrank you both and you are the only other officer up here, so that makes you the deputy, no?" Sciandretti waved at the second milk stool in the corner and said, "pull up a chair and I'll make you smarter on our campaign plans."

O'Connell did as he was told and listened carefully as Sciandretti outlined a two-month plan of harassment operations across the entire region down the Tiber almost to Rome.

"Good thing we have those boots coming, O'Connell. We are going to be doing a fair bit of walking."

28 March 1944. Panjim Harbor, Portuguese Colony of Goa

Steinmark sat in his home overlooking Panjim port. He had just finished decoding a message from Berlin. Now he focused on the challenges implied in the message. The internal conflicts inside the Nazi party and the German military had finally reached out and touched him. He had to decide what he was going to do about it.

As he rubbed his temple near his missing eye he wondered about his career. He volunteered for the Brandenburgers to get free from the Eastern Front and the catastrophe of Operation *BARBAROSSA*. At the start of the Eastern Front, he was a German cavalry officer in the Ukraine. He saw the war from the commander's position in the turret of his six-wheeled *Panzershawagen* racing ahead of the advancing tank divisions searching for the best routes with the least possible resistance. Once the Soviet line held firm in Russia proper, the war became less and less a conflict of maneuver and more and more a static slaughterhouse. Steinmark had been a young soldier in the first war on the Italian Front under the command of a young officer named Erwin Rommel. Rommel's work in Italy was designed to keep the troops mobile, but static combat was the nature of that war. Steinmark had no intention of living in a trench in this war waiting for the next artillery barrage to kill him.

Brandenburg Division operations on the Eastern Front were known to be dangerous, audacious and highly mobile. He volunteered for the Division and was sent to the training academy at Brandenburg Kaserne. When the instructor cadre found out that he spoke excellent Italian along with Spanish and Portuguese, after the completion of his training his orders sent him to North Africa instead of back to the Eastern Front. While the North African desert with heat, limited water and flies was hardly a paradise, Steinmark was happy to be sleeping soundly in the desert rather than in the cold of Russia where you could easily have your throat slit in your sleep by a Soviet Partisan. But, the operation in Palestine ended all of that.

Steinmark had never been a Nazi. He was a loyal member of the German Army and committed to Germany. As a soldier in 1939, he had taken the oath to support Hitler, but that was only because it was an order from the German Army leadership. The Nazi party left him cold with their fake military honors, their political drama and their ridiculous Aryan ideology. As an officer first on the Eastern Front and then in the Brandenburger Division, Steinmark had faced more challenges than most of the self-absorbed Nazi party members in Berlin would face in a lifetime. Their petty competitions and fancy uniforms had meant very little to him. But now, he faced a challenge that required him to think through precisely how he would survive a political threat instead of a military threat. At the thought of his Brandenburger days, Steinmark touched the eyepatch which covered the empty socket where his right eye used to be. The eyepatch was as much a talisman as it was physical reminder of a bad and violent day. After his success over the last two years, now he suddenly faced a challenge that had nothing to do with his work and everything to do with his ability to report accurately but not necessarily completely to the Nazi hierarchy.

The message he just deciphered came from the Reich Main Security Office, the Nazi Party security enterprise. They made it clear that they were now running Germany's intelligence operations and the Abwehr had been disbanded. Steinmark had heard on the BBC radio broadcasts that the Abwehr had been in conflict with the Nazis, but he assumed it was all propaganda. Now, he was not so sure. What was certain was the message was signed by a new commander, SS Brigadier Walter Schellenberg. Under his name was the title commander followed by the term *Ausland SD* — "Overseas Security Service". It annoyed Steinmark that he had spent time deciphering Schellenberg's name and then his job title.

In the Abwehr, no message had ephemera. Deciphering messages using a one-time code pad was an exercise in frustration. Adding extra letters just to send a signature block was the sort of thing Steinmark expected from senior Nazis. All he knew for sure was Schellenberg had a reputation in Berlin as a Nazi stooge who advanced by two means: As a sycophant to his superiors and as a brutal task master to his subordinates. The message stated that he was to remain in place, continue on his established mission, but to stand by to obey additional, sensitive orders from the Nazi Party. Steinmark could only imagine what sort of corrupt orders he might receive from a Nazi functionary. No wonder Germany had lost North Africa and was losing on the Eastern Front. Nazi Party leadership. Shit.

O'Connell and his team worked South along the Apennines harassing small German patrols, killing Italian Fascists who were still trying to exert control over the villages, and generally making themselves an annoyance to anyone not supporting the allied cause. All along the route, Carlo Guido had served as his translator, travel guide and single English speaking companion. Over time, O'Connell had gained fitness and now could hold a real conversation while they walked. What he learned made him aware of the nature of his resistance partners.

"We go tonight to a place that used to be owned by my uncle. Fascists drove him off the farm in 1935 so a local Fascisti could add his property. When my uncle resisted, they killed him, his wife and their children."

"What did you do?"

"We waited until we had the means to do something…I think my teachers in Boston would use the word sublime."

"Sublime?"

"Beautiful."

"Thank you, Carlo. I know what sublime means." Carlo turned to the team and said something in Italian and they all laughed. "Another joke?"

"We all think you are very fun to talk to, Peter."

Four months into his deployment, O'Connell's uniform no longer resembled his original Army-issue wool. As to his original OSS kit, he only had his Bulova watch and his weapons left. He was carrying his M1 folding-stock carbine and his .45 in a leather shoulder holster along with his fighting knife, a sleeve knife in a sheath on his left forearm and in one of his pockets what they called at the Farm a "cosh," which was nothing more than a rubber handle wrapped around a heavy duty spring with a steel ball at the end. He wore a mix of farm clothes, German captured equipment and his heavily repaired Army issue, olive drab wool shirt.

The last remnants of his original military uniform included the faded red beret given to him by his SOE parachute school instructors and his leather flying jacket. Completing his new uniform were a pair of Italian Army mountaineering boots. As Sciandretti warned, he had to give up his US jump boots when a supply drop did not deliver as promised. That night, his partisan team leader, Anthony Guido, who had been the recipient of O'Connell's boots arrived with the pair of boots. "Too big for me," was all Anthony could say as he laughed a deep basso profundo laugh and walked away to relate yet another story of the crazy American.

His leather flying jacket with US flag issued just before he jumped into Italy now looked as if it had been dragged miles behind a truck. In fact, at one point it had been dragged as he tried to sabotage a German Mercedes cargo truck by cutting the brake lines just as the truck headed down a mountain pass. It was parked when he crawled under the vehicle, but it pulled away from the brief stop on the road and O'Connell held on for a hundred yards until he knew he was clear of his team. His goal was to ensure that if he was caught, he would appear to be a single American airman evading capture rather than an American OSS agent running partisan operations. In the end, the truck's brake lines did fail, and the cargo truck ended up on its side at the bottom of the pass. Little of value in the truck, but another success for the Partisans.

The Partisans told and retold the story — with considerable laughter — at every stop along the way. They appreciated his commitment to their safety but agreed the American was *pazzo*, crazy, to risk himself for them. Carlo said, "Now you are a true brother, a true member of the communist brotherhood, Peter. We will fight and die together."

O'Connell said, "Carlo, we will fight together but I'm going to do my best to make sure we don't die together."

Carlo translated and family Guido once again said in unison, "Bravo, American!"

O'Connell looked through his binoculars at the bridge crossing the River Liri. The captured German optics were at least twice as good as anything he ever used in the US Army. He could see the bridge with its German Army guards, the stone arches, and the river below filled with melt water from snow that still covered the tops of the Abruzzi Mountains. The bridge was part of the large resupply network for German units along the Gustav Line which served as the German defensive positions south of Rome. This was the Partisans' next objective and certainly the most important. O'Connell watched as trucks of every shape and size hauled supplies, fuel and occasionally replacement tanks heading toward the battle-lines near Monte Cassino. He backed away from his observation post and returned to the Partisans, waiting in a small cave on the south side of the foothills below the Abruzzi Mountains.

O'Connell started the debriefing using Carlo Guido as his translator. "Carlo, please tell your cousin and his men that we need to destroy the bridge tonight. It will cripple the Germans and Fascist and open the way for our forces to capture Roma." Carlo nodded and addressed the twenty Partisans. After he finished, O'Connell continued, "I think the best way to do this is to attack a convoy as it is on the bridge while we also dynamite one of the bridge arches."

As Carlo did the translation, O'Connell noticed a rapid and emotional discussion among the ranks. It was the first time he saw something resembling disagreement, so he asked Carlo to explain.

"They say the bridge is Roman and it is the only bridge like it across the Liri. They think the Germans would simply create a new bridge using their equipment and we would lose this heritage and our ability to move our own supplies across the river. They have another idea." Carlo nodded as he spoke making it clear that O'Connell absolutely needed to listen to the alternative.

O'Connell responded, "I want to hear it because blowing the bridge would be hard."

"They say we should take the bridge and hold it long enough to destroy the road where it curves past the outcrop a few hundred meters south. If we do that, there will be a halt while the Germans try to engineer something. Traffic will be backed up for many kilometers and your Air Force will attack the convoys. It will delay for much longer.

Small scale demolition had been the team's stock and trade, but destroying a road seemed a stretch. O'Connell asked, "Do they know how to destroy the road?"

Carlo pointed to one of the oldest men on the team. "My uncle Mario says he helped make that road cut twenty years ago and he can drop the cliff with four sticks of dynamite. He just needs the dynamite and no interruptions. That is why my cousin, Anthony," Carlo nodded to the partisan leader, "says we need to take the bridge and hold it long enough that everyone fights us, and Mario can do his marvel."

After months with this team, O'Connell knew that once they made up their minds on how a job was to be accomplished, it made no sense to try to fight that tide. He had learned over time that the Partisans often had a better way. And, who knew that "Uncle Mario" was a construction engineer? It wasn't as if he had biographic information on anyone and they wouldn't have told him if he had asked. O'Connell nodded and said, "It is a good plan. Anthony will lead from the south, I will lead from the north, and Mario and one other will have a half hour to do the necessary demolition. Agreed?"

The team nodded and quickly divided up after passing a bottle of grappa around for one last drink. The bridge attack would begin at midnight exactly. Nine of the partisans, including Carlo went with O'Connell. Anthony lead his team and his two demolition experts to a footbridge of the Liri used only by farmers. They had the longer walk so they left at a brisk pace. Before they left, O'Connell and Anthony synchronized their watches. Anthony was wearing a German pilot's watch that he said he "found" early in the war. Given all the other things that the Partisans had "found" over the past two months, O'Connell was not surprised that many of them wore German watches on their wrists and fine German daggers on their belts.

The approach to the north side of the bridge was relatively easy. There were a series of small gullies that fed into the river near the bridge. While spring had yet to arrive in the mountains, here in the Liri Valley the trees were starting to leaf and shoots from previously planted grain were turning the fields from dirt brown to green. The team moved along these gullies in ankle deep water, using nothing more than the light of a waxing moon and the sound of the German convoys to guide them toward the bridge. Each of the two partisan squads had a captured German heavy machine gun and a *Panzer-faust* anti-tank weapon as well as their normal mix of rifles and captured German submachine guns. O'Connell helped place his team's machine gun to gain maximum firepower on the key targets from a small ridge line parallel to the road. Then, he took the rest of the team on their final approach to an area close to the road. Just as they arrived in their position at 2355hrs, O'Connell heard the fighting begin at the opposite end of the bridge. Carlo turned to O'Connell and shaking his head said, "Even when he was a kid, Anthony was impatient."

O'Connell didn't have time to reply as he started to run toward their attack position. Since all of the defenders of the bridge were focused on the opposite end of the bridge, his team was able to close in and begin the attack before the German guards or the lorry drivers realized there was an attack from the north as well. From the position above the road, the German general-purpose machine gun operated by O'Connell's team began its steady fire of six rounds, break, six rounds. This firing pattern was part of O'Connell's instructions to make sure the barrel of the gun did not overheat. Another benefit that he noticed was the sound of the German heavy machine gun firing in a disciplined way created relief among the German troops, at least until they realized that the gun was firing at them.

Along with being his translator, Carlo was the only one on O'Connell's team who knew how to use the *panzerfaust.* O'Connell pointed to a German tank transporter that was pulling a Panzer III main battle tank across the bridge. Carlo aimed and fired. The rocket propelled shaped charge entered the tank's rear deck and exploded. O'Connell never knew for sure whether the round created a secondary explosion in the tank's ammunition magazine or the fuel tank. Whatever the cause, the tank was lifted off the trailer and fell on its side blocking the road while rounds from the tank's magazine caused secondary explosions sending shrapnel in all directions.

His partisans were working along the various trucks trapped on the south side of the bridge. Just as he had trained the machine gunners, he drilled the rest of the team in fire discipline. O'Connell was glad to hear them use short bursts from their captured submachine guns. In the first few ambushes in February, the partisans fired until their German submachine guns jammed from the heat. Now, they were careful to use just enough firepower to kill the enemy while keeping enough ammunition available in case of a counterattack.

The counterattack came more quickly than anyone expected. There were two cargo trucks on the central span of the bridge when the attack started. They were filled with troops dressed in the dreaded black uniforms of the Nazi SS: Well trained, well fed, disciplined and ruthless. They jumped out of the trucks and began to move both north and south in controlled fire and maneuver. The only thing that kept them from overrunning the ambush in the first minutes of the attack was the effective fire from the two resistance machine guns at opposite ends of the bridge. Still, they seemed determined to win the fight and O'Connell could only hope Mario completed his job before the SS troops gained access to better cover behind the trucks stopped at either end of the bridge.

As if an answer to his prayers, at 0014hrs O'Connell heard the explosions south of the bridge followed by the sound of a landslide. First a few rocks and then the sound of a side of a mountain crashing down on the road. All of the Partisans cheered and, in good order, simply disappeared into the night. O'Connell was the last to leave the fight at the bridge as he counted heads as his men passed from the road to the gully and back into the mountains. He turned to look one last time at the destruction when he realized he was staring at the moon and the stars. He couldn't remember falling. He knew he was on his back in the cold stream that they had followed to the bridge. It was very cold. And he was very tired.

10 June 1944, Panjim Harbor, Portuguese Colony of Goa

Steinmark shut off the short wave radio. He had been listening to Radio Berlin. He had grown used to hearing the propaganda from Berlin and reading between the lines. Heroic efforts meant the Wehrmacht was retreating. The commitment to the Fatherland by the German people meant the allied bombings were severe. The strength of the Nazi Party meant the Nazi Party was collapsing. It was all shit.

He also listened to the BBC. The one thing he noticed over the years was the BBC reported on British defeats as well as British victories. While he was recuperating from his wounds in Potsdam, he listened to their reporting on North Africa. The battle of Tobruk was excellent news, but then it was disheartening when they started to report on defeat after defeat of the Afrika Corps. Disheartening because he knew they were telling the truth. Now the BBC was reporting that the Allies had landed in France and on the southern front they had captured Rome. There was plenty of opportunity for the Americans and the British to be defeated on the battlefield, but it was clear to Steinmark, the tide had turned against Germany.

Just before he listened to the Radio Berlin broadcast, he listened to his own shortwave link with the latest message from the Reich Main Security Office. The ciphered message instructed Steinmark to redouble his efforts against the British Navy in Bombay. That was no surprise, though he doubted he could accomplish the mission. Of course, the orders from Schellenberg also said that he had to do so with no new supply of funds. So, short of swimming into Bombay harbor and planting limpet mines on British ships, he doubted there was much more he could do. There was no question that Mr. Golpani was highly motivated by his payments, but Golpani was not willing to sacrifice his entire criminal enterprise for Steinmark's gold. In any event, the source reporting he had coming out of Bombay said that the Royal Navy shipping had shifted priorities and ships were headed primarily to Australia. Steinmark didn't care whether the British won or lost to the Japanese and taking additional risks might affect his only goal: To make sure India didn't help the British Army defeat Germany.

Steinmark was a loyal German officer but he was also a realist. As he watched the page of his ciphered message burn in his ash tray, he wondered how long he could or even should work for the Nazi regime. He received a letter the previous week from his Abwehr colleague who managed the Rio de Janeiro end of the Abwehr cover company. Oberleutnant Klaus von Bingen was another wounded war veteran who Canaris used for the Abwehr. He had been an executive officer on a U-boat who lost his left leg in September 1940 during a torpedo run against a British destroyer. After he recovered and was fitted with his new prosthetic, Canaris dispatched him to Brazil in 1942 as Dom Miguel Bonaferes. As Bonaferes, he used Abwehr funds to create the import-export firm MERCURY CORPORACAO.

Von Bingen's hand-written note had taken nearly a month to arrive from Brazil by way of Portugal and carried in one of the company's locked mail bags. It was written in Portuguese and filled with cover names and double-talk. Two points had hit Steinmark the hardest. First, the note implied that Admiral Canaris was under house arrest and would be tried for treason. Treason! Steinmark shook his head. Admiral Canaris dedicated his life to Germany first as a submarine commander and then as an intelligence officer. That the Nazis could accuse him of treason was insufferable. The second point was equally difficult to accept. Von Bingen said he was going to "quit the company" and move to Panama. The note closed with a simple comment that Steinmark should think about his own future because the company would likely go bankrupt within the year. Steinmark wondered if his company was already bankrupt.

>>>>>> JEDBURGH

01 July 1944, 0230hrs. Southern France.

The smell of aviation gas permeated everything inside the small airplane. Peter O'Connell, Clive Barker, and Francois Broumand were crammed into the back of the Lysander aircraft filled with rucksacks, weapons and ammunition. They were shoulder to shoulder inside the tail of the aircraft with only a small piece of the pilot's windscreen visible to give them any sense of where they were. Mostly, that view was of silver gray night sky. O'Connell looked at the radium dial on his Bulova watch. It was 0230hrs. If the pilot briefing was correct, they were somewhere over the Mediterranean and headed into Southern France. Jedburgh team CRANKCASE was on its way to engage the French resistance near Avignon.

For a single engine aircraft, the Lysander was a powerful delivery tool of special operations. It was able to land in farmer's fields and with external fuel tanks, it had long range, though long range at a slow speed. This particular plane had seen some hours. It was stitched together along the fuselage and the control cables that ran along the length of the aircraft were leaking grease. O'Connell was not entirely sure in the darkness, but he thought he could see through the skin of the aircraft where either machine gun fire or shrapnel had cut through on some previous flight. The plane smelled of oil and sweat. The sweat was from the three members of the Jedburgh team. They were flying low over the Mediterranean and the summer warmth coupled with fear prior to any insertion to make a body sweat.

It had been an eventful three months since the attack on the Liri River bridge. After recovering in Cairo from a bullet wound in his shoulder, O'Connell had expected to return to Italy. By the time he was fit for duty, Rome had been captured, the Germans were retreating toward the Alps and James Sciandretti and his Italian Partisans were conducting what was called in polite company "stabilization" operations. That meant the resistance in the Apennines were hunting Fascist sympathizers and re-starting old feuds. O'Connell was needed elsewhere.

O'Connell also missed the invasion of France on the beaches of Normandy. He read newspaper reports about his old unit in the 82nd Airborne operating behind the lines. Their support for the landings at Utah Beach were said to have made the landing possible. He also read about the severe fighting on Omaha Beach. He had no idea what, if any, role OSS had in the operation. All he knew was he had missed the two most important operations in the war so far: the capture of Rome and invasion of France.

When Cairo command offered him an assignment in the next stage of operations in France, Operation DRAGOON, he grabbed the opportunity with both hands. DRAGOON was the invasion of Southern France and it was the first time that the OSS Special Operations was going to deploy a new team concept. The plan was to deploy three-man teams made up of one American, one British and one Free French special operator behind German lines. These "Jedburgh" teams, named after a town in the Scottish borderlands, were a new experiment in special operations. The teams were uniformed representatives of the Allies dropped in advance of conventional operations. They wore their uniforms with insignia and rank as a demonstration of their role as pathfinders for a larger allied force. Previously, the SOE and OSS sent a single agent plus a communicator to work with the resistance. Now, they were in country to show the resistance that allied armies were on their way and to encourage the resistance to attack specific, strategic targets to assist the campaign. This time, the objective was to guide the French resistance in a manner that would support the larger invasion force. O'Connell honestly didn't care how, he just wanted to get back into the fight.

He leaned over and shouted over the engine noise into the left ear of his British counterpart. It was the only way to hear anything in the aircraft, if you heard a voice even then. "Clive, thanks for liberating this aircraft for us. I thought we were going to have to arrange a jump into Avignon and that thought was not pleasant."

"No dramas, mate. The pilot had just returned from a cargo delivery in Italy and seemed up for a trip to France. We had the right moonlight and a promised reception committee. All good. Still, I know you have gone through the Joe Hole before in Italy, so why the concern about a jump into Avignon?"

Memories revolved in Peter's head. A dozen jumps including two combat jumps were more than enough for Peter O'Connell. The combat jumps were so alike that he almost found it possible that pilots hated paratroopers. The insertion into Sicily when he was still with the 504th, then his first OSS jump to meet with the Italian resistance. It was always the same. An unpleasant aircraft ride where you were desperate to get out of the plane before you puked, the rough opening shock of the parachute, the quiet ride to the ground and then the confusion in the dark as you tried to figure out where you were. At least he had never lost his boots or kit in the opening shock. Several of his paratroopers had lost boots, rifles, even helmets in Sicily. Of course, they were loaded with ammunition, rations and heavy weapons when the jumped out of the Dakotas, carrying nearly double the weight that was the safe limit of the parachute.

Barker interrupted his thoughts, "The last time I jumped into France, they put me 5 kilometers off target and I ended up sitting on about 500 pounds of equipment in a forest clearing waiting to see who would find me first — the Resistance or the Germans. I did not want a repeat of that performance. Also, I had no interest in trying to teach our French cavalry captain how to parachute into France in one week. He doesn't seem the type to take guidance well and I really didn't want to have to carry him off the dropping zone with a broken leg. A Lysander delivers you to the appointed place or you return to base. No other options."

Barker looked over at his French counterpart who was leaning against the bulkhead in a way designed to minimize the amount of grease he might get on his perfectly creased uniform. "He is a piece of work, that one. Do you think he has any idea what working with the resistance is going to be like?"

"Does anyone on their first trip in?" O'Connell reached up to touch the scar from the bullet wound in his left shoulder. His partisans had risked their lives to recover him from the ambush site and then carry him across the mountains to a coastline where they loaded him on the small fishing boat owned by another branch of the Guido family. Eventually it linked up with a US Navy submarine and he was taken back to Cairo. He was in a Cairo hospital four days after the ambush only because of the risks his Italian "communists" took to keep him alive.

"How long before we land?" Captain Francois Broumand of the Free French Army had finally opened his eyes and shouted into O'Connell's left ear ending his memories. In the dark, it was hard to tell, but he thought the French captain looked green.

O'Connell looked back at his watch and said, "Twenty minutes, I think."

Broumand returned to his careful lean against the bulkhead and his rucksack. No sense in continuing either discussion. The noise and the dark made conversation impossible. O'Connell was left to his thoughts on their mission and his partners. He knew Barker had experience in Greece and in France. He had been in SOE since 1941 and survived multiple rotations behind the lines. His SOE circuit *MIDLANDS* had operated in Calais. He heard from OSS/Cairo that Barker was good at what he did (explosives and radio operations) and avoided on things that he didn't like which meant he didn't try to sort out or even understand the internal politics of resistance groups. He would be reliable and steady in Avignon.

Broumand was an unknown. He had fought the Germans in 1940 from the commander's position in his tank right to the end of the

French fight. Apparently brave and audacious, he had two tanks destroyed out from under him before he was evacuated off the beach. He had spent the last three and a half years working with General De Gaulle's staff in the Free French Army. O'Connell was not entirely certain how Broumand would handle the fact that the French resistance in Southern France was not an army and not necessarily friendly to De Gaulle. Broumand was also not trained in radio communications, DZ operations or even small unit tactics. It would be interesting to see what he would be good for as a member of their JEDBURGH team other than serving as the representative of the Free French. Perhaps that was all he was there for anyhow.

Barker leaned his head against the skin of the aircraft and nodded into a light doze. This was his third trip behind the lines in the past two years. He knew that once on the ground, they would get very little rest for the first two or three days. Resistance movements were always "pleased" to see Allied representatives, but mostly they were pleased to see arms, ammunition and money. They tolerated the SOE because the SOE provided those three ingredients essential to fighting their war against the Germans and any local collaborators. Once they arrived in Southern France, it would take work to learn the internal rivalries of this resistance leadership. Barker figured it was still better than clearing minefields while serving in the Royal Green Jackets as a platoon commander of sappers. At least in the SOE, you could choose your own fate behind the lines so long as you didn't get your throat slit by the Resistance.

Almost exactly on time, the young RAF captain looked over his shoulder and shouted to the back of the airplane. Like most RAF pilots Barker worked with, he looked about 17 except for the dark circles under his eyes. His leather jacket with the sheepskin lining looked as if it would be in tatters soon and he had an unlit pipe jammed into his mouth. "About to get a bit dodgy, mates. Please do not bag up in my aircraft. "

O'Connell turned to Barker and said, "Bag up?"

"I suppose he means it will be bit of a rough approach and he doesn't want you to get sick in his aircraft. They hate it when you jump out leaving them to smell vomit for hours and then clean up when they get home. Most unfair, since they rarely have much of a ground crew." Barker barely had this comment out of his mouth when the aircraft rapidly dipped to the right and the tail seemed to be trying to meet up with the propeller.

Broumand squeezed his eyes tight closed and tried to keep from getting sick as the plane moved in directions and speed that he thought would surely pull the aircraft apart. This was his first trip back into France since 1940. Up till now, his job as a staff officer managing resistance circuits in Normandy from the Free French headquarters in London had involved selection of candidates who were sent to the SOE schools. Whether they returned or not had never been his business. He was a cavalry officer and cavalry was the honorable profession in the French Army. He had grown up knowing that he would follow in his father's footsteps as a French *hussar*. He had fought with two different tank crews in his squadron of six tanks. It was violent, bloody fighting. He was surprised as anyone that he made it to the beaches. After Dunkirk, he had been forced to give up his steel charger and join the French General staff in London. After some time on General De Gaulle's personal staff, he was assigned as liaison to the SOE, tasked with ensuring the right sort of French exile was selected for insertion back into France. That right sort of French exile needed to be a French exile who supported De Gaulle.

Broumand arrived at the base in Tunis along with a dozen other senior French officers in preparation for the invasion of Southern France: Operation DRAGOON. The French officers remained together for the first few days until selected for various missions. Broumand linked up with the OSS/SOE compound in Tunis in June while headquarters worked with the RAF and USAAF to determine what aircraft would be available to take them into Avignon. The first week after the capture of Rome and the invasion in Normandy, they were told that regular lift aircraft were not available. Barker used some connections to bring a Lysander first to Tunis and then to Corsica that allowed a direct flight into the area north of Avignon.

Both O'Connell and Barker were experienced, but neither was particularly interested in the future governance of France. They saw the mission from the perspective of the defeating the Germans. Broumand viewed it differently. The General made it clear to Broumand when he departed London that this was the final battle for the creation of a new France. A France led by De Gaulle and the Free French Army. Broumand's job was to make sure Avignon was part of that new France.

The aircraft crabbed sideways across the sky losing altitude along the way. Through the front windscreen, they could see sky, then ground, then sky, then ground slicing at a 45 degree angle across the windscreen and then, briefly, a set of small fires running perpendicular to their apparent flight route. After the last set of dramatic shifts, Barker commented, "Francois, mate, you have the right idea. Keep your eyes closed; having them open certainly doesn't help."

Broumand's comment was lost in the noise as the wheels hit the ground. The aircraft bounced along the farm field before the tail wheel finally hit the ground and the pilot feathered the prop while hitting the right wheel brake. One final skid, a 180 degree spin and then all movement stopped.

"All present and correct?" The pilot looked pleased with the landing and wanted them to get out of his airplane. O'Connell crawled over the equipment, opened the left side door and rolled out on the ground. Now they needed to sort out which faction of the resistance was serving as their reception committee. They had agreed that O'Connell would exit the aircraft first and make contact. If there were no problems, the other two would begin to unload the plane. If there were problems, O'Connell would be responsible for keeping any hostiles at bay while the pilot revved the engines and took off (with or without O'Connell, but at least with the other two Jedburghs).

A dozen men approached in the dark. They were dressed in a mix of farm clothes and old military field coats from the Great War. The only common feature was they were all wearing berets. Their weapons were at least as diverse as their clothing. They had shotguns, hunting rifles, captured German Mausers. They were also carrying pistols, knives and small axes stuffed into work belts. In the dark, they looked almost exactly like the image O'Connell remembered from an Andrew Wyeth illustration of *Treasure Island* from his childhood. They approached him in a rolling gait over the furrows in the farm field. The largest of these pirates grabbed and hugged him.

"Welcome to France, welcome my friend." He spoke in a French dialect that O'Connell could barely understand after his short language course while recuperating in Cairo. Peter looked back at the aircraft and waved. His two partners began to unload the cargo, explosives first, then two long boxes of rifles and ammunition. Not enough of anything, but a token of support. Hopefully, enough to begin the relationship. Once on the ground and able to communicate with the joint headquarters, they could arrange additional parachute drops of more of the same.

In previous deployments, SOE learned it was always appropriate for an officer to be at least a Lieutenant Colonel if he was going to have any reasonable conversation with a resistance leader who was always a "general." So, Major Peter O'Connell was wearing the British paratrooper smock with the rank of full colonel and Captain Clive Barker was wearing the lieutenant colonel rank. Broumand had been unwilling to change his rank and equally irritated that he had to work with these allies in a joint operation. He remained Captain Broumand of the Free French army and wore his officer's uniform with a degree of care that did not show with O'Connell or Barker. He was confident that the resistance would recognize him as the true leader of this team once they met in daylight.

As soon as the aircraft was empty, the pilot gave a quick wave, throttled the Lysander to full force and thundered down the field and was away. All told, he had been on the ground no more than five minutes, a few minutes more than he had requested, but probably not enough to put him at too great a risk. The black Lysander disappeared into the night sky and the fires on the edge of the field were extinguished. For the three Jedburghs, this was the first time it had been silent in over two hours. They were stunned by the still and the darkness.

The largest pirate grabbed O'Connell by the shoulder and shouted in his ear. "Time to go. The men will deliver the equipment. We go to meet our comrades to discuss operations. *Allez!*"

The Jedburghs grabbed their rucksacks, unslung their newly issued Thompson submachine guns, and followed the resistance representative across the field. They were running perpendicular to the furrows in the field, so quickly the pace became one of several quick steps followed by a stumble, a recovery, and then quick steps again. It was not the most graceful entrance you could imagine, but far better than anything Peter enjoyed before in Italy.

Resistance Base Camp - Avignon 25 July 1944

O'Connell and Barker were sitting next to the radio, having just received burst communication from OSS/SOE headquarters in Rome. It took about a half hour to break out the coded message using the one time pad they carried. O'Connell had a better "fist" and did the transmitting. Barker was better at taking down the Morse code and then decoding the messages. It also gave them an excuse every day to sit apart from the French resistance and Captain Broumand.

Barker read the message, "It says: *target 1-4 to be completed NLT 14 August. Transmit needed supplies NLT 28 July. Delivery at DZ on 09 August at 0345hrs. Safety signal arrow facing down DZ. Confirm receipt.*"

O'Connell tapped out *RR* answering roger, roger and started taking down the radio. The next transmission would be a long one so they would have to move the radio to a new location well away from their base camp. The local observers in Avignon reported to the resistance that there was Nazi radio direction finding equipment in town. Anything more than a few seconds could be just enough for them to fix a position.

"What are we going to do with Broumand?" O'Connell asked as he started to take down the radio. It was not a conversation he wanted to have, but it was needed.

"He is a bloody pill, no doubt. I thought his effort to lead the resistance fighters in *le Marsailles* and then reading De Gaulle's message to the resistance went well, don't you think?"

"If you mean they didn't kill him right there and then, yes, I thought it went as well as can be expected. I was afraid the communists would start singing the Communist International."

Shortly after arrival, O'Connell and Barker realized that most of their Resistance groups were communists. There were three main factions. One group were farmers from the area. One group were former Avignon trade unionists who had little sympathy for anyone from Paris and especially anyone from the DeGaulle faction, meaning the conservatives of the French Army. The third group were clearly Free French, conservative Catholic land owners. None of these resistants were soldiers by trade. Broumand appeared at first to be clueless that all of the fighters did not embrace his brand of politics. To him, DeGaulle was a charismatic symbol who represented the traditions of the French Army and the future of France. Broumand was especially frustrated when the local leadership kept coming to his American and British counterparts for advice and to ask for support. He felt snubbed by the Resistance and betrayed by the members of his team.

As they were wrapping up the last of the antenna wire, Broumand walked up and confronted O'Connell. "It is time for me to take command. I need to turn this rabble into an army before the invasion."

"Nuts."

"Excuse?"

"Simple English, pal. Crazy. These guys don't want to be and won't ever be soldiers. We don't want soldiers anyhow. We want saboteurs and subversives. It was the same for me in Italy and I suspect the same with Clive in Calais. Our soldiers are coming by way of DRA-GOON. Our job is to maximize the chaos just before DRAGOON. We don't need soldiers to do that. It's just a distraction."

"And after DRAGOON?"

"If DRAGOON succeeds, we leave and go to the next fight. The resistance fighters go back to being farmers and factory workers. We take the next job to defeat the Nazis. Maybe France, maybe Italy, maybe Germany. Beats me. If DRAGOON fails, we stay here and continue the chaos."

"And the future of France?"

"Buddy, that's up to Frenchmen like these guys and like you after we get the Nazis out of your country. I'm here to beat the Nazis."

"You Americans, you are such cowboys. Just like your cinema, only white hats, black hats. No history." Broumand offered the last comment over his shoulder as he left.

Barker came forward just as Broumand stumped off. He put his hands on his hips and assumed his most formal pose and spoke in his most ridiculous French accented English. "You Americans are such cowboys."

10 August 1944 - DZ Whiskey

The twelve parachutes were visible in the night sky as the pair of black painted B24 liberators disappeared to the south. Jacques' DZ reception committee was already putting out the signal fires they had lighted just before the aircraft arrived and it looked like the drop would be perfect. They had tried for 09 August, but weather was poor. This would be the last window for drops before DRAGOON. On the edge of the DZ, three separate groups from the local resistance were waiting for the weapons, ammunition and demolitions to land.

The three Jedburghs waited at the north end of the DZ preparing to manage the distribution of the material. DZ operations were complex in the best of times and working with three groups in the dark made it more complicated still. Each of the resistance groups considered itself to be the most important in the area. The Jedburghs had debated how to manage the distribution. At first, they thought to take the loads to a secondary location and then split the material, but none of the resistance leaders accepted this option. They assumed there would be too much pilfered before the distribution.

Barker watched as the last parachute drifted below the tree line. He said, "Alright, mate. Tell me again how we manage this circus?"

O'Connell said, "Clive, you take Jacques' bunch and move to the south end of the DZ and start opening the last four bundles. Francois, you take Jocelyn's bunch and do the same for the middle four and

I will take Henri's team here and start south. If the OSS packers followed our instructions and we are lucky with the winds, I reckon everyone gets what they want. OK?"

Broumand shook his head and said, "Peter, I agree, but it will be complicated."

"Too bloody right, Francois, but we have to let the locals sort this out themselves." Broumand shook his head and took off at a dead run to the group in the middle of the drop zone.

Once he was out of hearing, O'Connell said to Barker, "I let him work with Jocelyn what more could he want?"

"Peter, you realize Jocelyn's group are communists, right?"

"What difference does that make? He has worked with them before and he has been making moon eyes at their leader since we first met them last month."

"Fingers crossed, mate." Barker took off on a run to the far end of the DZ as the first of his bundles landed.

For the next half hour, O'Connell supervised the recovery of the four bundles designated for Henri's group. Luck was with them and the four bundles were equal distributions of British Sten submachine guns and ammunition, two American .30 caliber machine guns and belted ammunition and a full bundle of explosives. The fourth bundle included detonation cord and "time pencil" detonators wrapped in a bale of cotton to prevent accidental detonation. Henri was pleased and managed the work with care, not bad for a dairy farmer who, prior to the war, had never been a leader and never fired anything but a shotgun. He had the weapons and equipment off the drop zone and had recovered the canvas bundles and parachutes in record time.

Barker walked up to O'Connell and smiled, "This is the twentieth load in the last three year that I have received by parachute. It's the first time it landed on the DZ and in the right order. Jacques' kit is all present and correct and he is already moving out to the rendezvous at his base camp. He didn't like sharing the shipment, but that's just Jacques, eh?"

O'Connell said, "They don't like each other on principle and definitely don't like sharing weapons. I always wonder how many they stash away for some future civil war."

"Peter, they are villains. You can be sure at least a quarter of the load is held back for the future. Of course, if they make good use of the other three quarters, I reckon they are more efficient than any conventional army."

"Too true. Shall we head down to Jocelyn and Francois?"

As they walked down the drop zone, they passed the last of Henri's team recovering the parachutes. Jocelyn's team was doing the same. Jocelyn's team called themselves communists, but their level of comradeship did not translate into cooperation. As a group, they were not as good as the farmers and smugglers that made up Henri and Jacques' forces. Peter wondered if they had thought about Marx at all when they signed up for communism. Communism might be better understood as an ideal rather than a practice for Jocelyn's mix of unionists, teachers, and writers.

Jocelyn greeted them. She was dressed in worker's coveralls, a leather vest and beret. A bandolier across her chest and a Mauser rifle in her left hand. She was eighteen. She became the leader of this group when her father was killed in an ambush in 1942. The local Soviet had elected her and she had proved to be an even better leader than her father. Next to her stood her deputy, a dockworker from Marseilles who went by the name Negat. O'Connell wasn't sure if Negat just had a natural sour personality or if he just hated Americans.

"Acceptable, comrade?" O'Connell tried to greet her as Jocelyn once and based on her response at that time and Negat's sneer, he never tried again.

"Acceptable, but always we have to share with those others who never fight. Where is the justice?"

"Only when we are done with the Nazis." Barker was always quick with the right comment in the right dialect of French.

"Where is Francois, comrade?"

"I did not see him after we arrived here. I thought he was with you."

"We need to find him so we can leave."

They started working along the DZ, asking Jocelyn's men as they passed from bundle to bundle. They found their French partner on the north boundary between the deliveries for Jocelyn's and Jacques' groups. He was dead in the middle of the drop zone. A bundle weighing about 250 pounds was resting on the body. His neck broken and his arm crushed. Jocelyn arrived just as they uncovered his body.

"What happened?"

"It appears a bundle hit him as he was running over to your team."

"Poor Francois, poor man."

"Comrade, get your men to recover this bundle and bring one of the canvas covers for Francois. We will take care of him."

As she left, Barker looked at O'Connell and said, "He was a dim sod, for sure, but he didn't die on a dropping zone. Especially given the cause of death."

O'Connell was squatting near Broumand's body. He looked up at Barker and said, "Nope. He didn't deserve this sort of treachery. He was knifed under the ribs and then carried here. We have a murderer on this DZ. As long as that murderer thinks we don't know that, the safer we will be and the more likely we can catch him or her. We can't sort out anything here in the dark. We will take Francois to the base camp and try to sort this out in daylight"

"**T**his was the best you could come up with, mate?" Barker was rolling up the long cable antenna and placing it into the crate that housed the radio, key, batteries and the antenna. They had just finished sending the current update to London.

"I didn't see you offering any brilliance there, Sherlock. Look we have a couple of problems.."

"Really, only a couple? We are behind Nazi lines and we know they are trying to find us. We just told our headquarters that Francois was killed in a Dropping Zone accident..."

"Well, actually we said he was killed on the DZ. I never used the work accident."

"Don't quibble. We know someone murdered him, and the best you can offer is a plan to tell the three resistance leaders, who hate each other by the way, that one of them has a Nazi collaborator in their midst."

"I knew you would see the brilliance."

"Too true, mate. Brilliant." O'Connell and Barker were in a small clearing having just sent their scheduled burst communications to London. They had kept up the charade of Francois' accidental death with the Resistance and had buried him in a local Catholic cemetery after hours with the assistance of a priest who supported the Resistance. A team of Free French resistance fighters joined in the small ceremony which Peter ran after dark. It was no easy time. Afterward, they returned to one of the local farmhouses that served as a resistance safe house and toasted to Francois before Peter and Clive returned to their own hideaway in the forest. The leaders promised to redouble their sabotage efforts in honor of Francois. Even the communists seemed shaken by the randomness of the loss.

After meeting with the Resistance leaders in the morning, they were once again debating the next steps. The two remaining Jedburghs faced an entirely different dilemma. Was Broumand killed because of some personal feud? That was always a possibility in groups where personal loyalties, rivalries and vendettas operated just below the surface. An alternative theory was that the murder was part of a larger plan, most likely a Nazi plan, to kill all of the team. Barker believed the former and O'Connell believed the latter. The challenge was how to ferret out the truth while still focusing on their real mission: To disrupt Nazi operations in advance of DRAGOON.

Barker said, "What is the point of creating a potential witch hunt inside the groups, especially now? We have real work to do and internal chaos is not going to help."

"I hope to create just enough chaos inside the ranks that the traitor will expose himself."

"But what if there is no master plot here? What if it was just a Frenchman who was tired of Francois' political lectures? I don't see that sort of villain exposing himself."

O'Connell shook his head. "Fair enough. What do we do then?"

"We carry on, we watch out for each other and we do our job of creating chaos for the Nazis rather than creating chaos in the Resistance. If there is a traitor, the more chaos we create, the more likely he will reveal himself."

O'Connell didn't want argue any more. He was tired, Barker's points made sense, and the murder was something that might never be solved. O'Connell just hated to think that someone could murder one of the team and then walk away. "OK, I reckon you are right. We will just stick with the plan, but no more splitting up to help two resistance groups concurrently. We stay together. "

"See, even a Mick like you can recognize a good idea every so often, mate."

"Just remember, we watch our backs from now on because we can't trust any of these guys."

"I never did, mate. I barely trust you."

T he following days were successful. O'Connell and Barker provided the resistance groups with their missions and, based on the courier reports, the French were living up to their promise to dedicate their effort to Francois Broumand. The previous night, two German fuel dumps near Avignon were aflame and the entire telephone and telegraph exchange was down. The attacks were distributed across the region so the German command was forced to run troops across the countryside and couldn't focus on a single security effort to find and destroy the resistance.

It was sunset and O'Connell and Barker were in the back of a horse-drawn hay cart heading south with ten French farmers on one of the main roads to the coast. It was beautiful evening with blue sky giving way to mauve and the first of the stars were starting to come out. To any casual observer, they were harvesters trying to get one last bit of hay in before dark. The French "farmers" surrounded the two Jedburghs, their rucksacks, and the weapons of the entire team. As the final push in advance of DRAGOON, the team was going to drop the two bridges in the region that could hold heavy vehicles. The previous attacks were designed to move the Germans away from the bridges which were simple trestles across irrigation canals. The canals were ten feet wide and five feet deep and would serve as ideal tank obstacles. With the bridges gone, the German response to DRAGOON would be limited to whatever force was available on the day of the operation south of the canals. Tanks, tank destroyers, half-tracks and virtually any wheeled vehicles north of the canal would (o) not be able to join the fight only after the Germans created new bridges. The hope was that by the time new bridges were available, it would be too late.

Barker was the expert on this. He was a Royal Engineer by training and had a year of engineering college before the war. Five years of blowing up bridges and cratering roads in Yugoslavia, Greece and Northern France gave him enough experience to be quite creative. He turned to O'Connell as they approached their drop-off point. "Now, listen carefully, mate, because you are about to hear a bit of brilliance that you rarely hear from a man in uniform."

"Oh, you do go on and on, don't you."

"You are the only audience I have, so it's good you are so agreeable."

"It doesn't hurt that I can carry my share of explosives either…"

"Too right, mate. Now here is where the brilliance comes in. We are not going to blow the bridges."

"Eh?"

"No, my friend, we are not going to blow the bridges because the Germans would simply replace them with some engineering marvel from the Panzer division."

"So, why am I getting ready to carry thirty pounds of explosives along with my Tommy-gun ammo?"

"Because, young Peter, we are setting up a tripwire that sets off the explosives the first time a tank crosses the bridge, it collapses with tank and crew. Think of the mess!"

"Certain?"

"Oh, dear. Are you suggesting that you doubt my genius? Can it be that you have lost faith? Why do you think I had our French friends out measuring the bridges, wading in the water. Fishing, perhaps?"

"Calculating stress and strain?"

"Peter, just when I think you pay no attention to my lectures, you prove me wrong. Exactly. We are going to enhance the damage already on the bridges, make them weaker and ready to collapse under anything more than a freight wagon or a scout motorcycle. Then, when they decide to use the bridge to move the tanks, poof, goodbye Panzers. Oh, and the reason you are carrying the explosives is because I am carrying the detonators. Never mix and match."

The wagon crossed a farm field and rolled into the woods on the edge of the field. The "farmers" jumped off the hay wagon. The Jedburghs climbed out of their hiding place and handed the resistance fighters their Sten guns, carbines and the one mortar. O'Connell turned to Michel, the team leader and said, "Stay here and be prepared to leave at once if need be. Identify defensive positions if we have to fight. Clive and I are going forward to the bridges. We will be back by midnight. If we don't come back on schedule, assume we have been captured and leave the area and continue the fight. Michel, good luck."

The resistance fighter grabbed O'Connell and then Barker by the shoulders and said, "*Bon chance!*"

They pulled on the rucksacks and slung their Thompsons and headed into the woods on a due south azimuth. The farthest bridge over the irrigation canal was over two kilometers away through the forest. They would plant the explosives for this one first, then work their way back, rigging charges on the other bridge before returning to the RV location. After a very hot and unpleasant hour they reached the first target. This bridge was an old stone and wood trestle bridge. No guards, no locals appeared as they watched the target for another 30 minutes.

"What a shame to damage that piece of history. It must be well over 100 years old — maybe even from Napoleon's engineers. A real beauty."

"I'm sympathetic Clive, but I'm also ready to drop some of these charges off here, so shall we get on with it."

"Peter, you can be such a barbarian."

"So I've been told."

They cached the rucksacks and slowly worked along the canal to the bridge. Clive planted the charges, Peter served both as lookout and courier — providing wire, detonators and switches on demand. The last step was for Clive to run a double strand of steel wire across the bridge which would trigger the detonator. "This will cause the explosion when the vehicle goes over the bridge, like an anti-tank mine, right?"

"Give us a bit for sophistication. A musket and a Thompson are both guns, right?"

"Ok, professor, you made your point. Are we done here? I'm the one up to my crotch in irrigation water."

"One minute you are complaining about being too warm and when I arrange for you to have a bath, all I get is further noise from your gob. What is a mother to do?"

The second bridge was much like the first. They were done and walking through the darkness back to their rucksack cache with nearly an hour to spare and less than a kilometer back to the RV when Barker went down like he was punched in the jaw. He groaned, "Mate, I'm shot."

O'Connell crawled over to his Jedburgh partner. He opened his aid pack and put the pressure bandage on Barker's shoulder. "Hold this! I didn't hear the shot, did you?"

"Sorry, mate. I was too busy falling over."

"Germans don't use silencers. Germans don't need to use silencers."

At that point, they both heard the approach of a hunter stalking his prey. Slow and deliberate. Then a voice out of the shadows saying, "Gentlemen, you might as well accept the fact that you are dead men. The only question is how soon."

Another bullet passed near O'Connell's head. Another silent round though he heard the whine as it went by. Whoever was shooting at them was aiming for head shots. The shot that hit Barker in the top of the shoulder had only missed his head by a few inches. As he considered this, O'Connell also thought he recognized the voice. It was one of Jocelyn's lieutenants...Negat, perhaps. He was supposed to be well to the east with Jocelyn raiding a fuel dump.

O'Connell couldn't see anyone in the woods. The sniper was careful as well as deliberate. Barker looked at him and whispered, "Will you kill him for goodness sake?"

O'Connell rolled on his left side. He reached inside his paratrooper smock and pulled out the High Standard .22 fitted with the silencer. Another round cracked through the space between the two allies. He pulled the slide and put the pistol into battery. O'Connell remembered his OSS firearms instructor during training. "Gentlemen, the High Standard pistol is for close in work. Many of you have probably hunted with a .22 rifle. Our rounds are better than the rounds used for hunting rabbits, but even our .22 rounds can only bring down a man at 10 yards, and only then with a perfect shot. Any farther and you are simply wasting .22 ammunition. Too much closer, you might as well get closer and use your knife."

O'Connell understood. But first, he had to find the bastard. He moved again, this time away from Barker and another round went over his head. As he moved, he looked up to see if he could identify the flash. Even a suppressed weapon had some flash.

Another bullet fired. In an attempt to get the sniper to speak, Barker shouted, "You bastard. You blew his brains out."

"That was the idea, Britisher. Now I will come to make sure you are done as well." The assassin spoke in heavily accented English. Barker had heard the accent before. In Yugoslavia? Definitely not a French accent.

Out of the darkness, a man in an all-black camouflage suit appeared briefly against the shadows of the trees. He still moved cautiously. Even if the American was dead, the British agent was only wounded. His instructor had always reminded him. Do not approach the target until you are certain he is dead. In the dark, he was not certain where the Britisher was, but he was absolutely certain he was alive. He already had a round loaded in his silenced Moisin-Nagant rifle and he used the tree to balance the rifle while he scanned the grass using his telescopic scope.

"What are you waiting for, froggy? Come visit me." The Britisher's voice was helping but he needed more to find him. He had to get him to talk more.

"I am no Frenchman, you fool."

"German then…"

Nearly there. He needed just a bit more noise and that would be it. He brought the rifle up to his cheek and said, "Wrong again, Britisher. Soviet special services. I am here to ensure the French communists win the war after the Germans leave. You and your dead friends were in the way."

"A Russian?"

The suppressed round smacked into the skull with no more sound than a dart hitting a dart board.

O'Connell stood over the body of their adversary. Dressed in black. A black hood was now soaked in black blood from the first round fired from behind. He put another two rounds into the sniper's back, rolled him over with his foot, and put two more rounds into the assassin's head. He was not taking chances.

"If you are done over there, do you think you could come over here and provide some first aid?" Barker's voice rattled with pain.

O'Connell picked up the rifle and walked over to Barker. "Did you keep the compress on the wound, Mr. Smart guy while I was saving your life?"

"Yes, doctor. Did you make sure he was good and dead?"

O'Connell sat down in the tall grass, exhausted physically and emotionally. "It wasn't pretty."

"Close in never is. First time?"

"Yes. I've seen plenty of my pals dead and I have shot at Germans, but this is the first time I killed someone at this range." O'Connell paused for a deep breath and said, "Russians!? What the heck do Russians have to do with us?"

"If you had worked out of Bari like I have, you wouldn't be surprised. We saw this sort of rivalry in Yugoslavia and Albania. The

Russians are determined to control Europe after we win this war. They don't like interference and they play to win," Barker paused, "Peter, You realize we can't report this back to London?"

"Why not?"

"Peter, you really are a bit of a colonial ruffian. If we say we killed a Soviet in the woods because he was the murderer, about the same time London gets the message, so will Moscow. I don't know for certain, but I always assume they intercept and decrypt our messages. Why do you think Mr. Killer was here? Just by accident? Just in case? I really would prefer Moscow doesn't find out our comrade failed in his mission. One Russian killer per trip is all I can handle."

"So, we bury him now and wait until we are debriefed when we return?"

"First, you take care of my shoulder. Then you bury him. And then, assuming we live through the rest of this holiday to Southern France, we sort out when and how we are going to report this."

Steinmark should have been enjoying a glass of wine on his patio while watching the sun set. Instead, he was inside his warehouse, at a desk illuminated by a pair of green shaded lamps. He was checking the books, alone at the end of the day. MERCURY CORPORACAO had never been designed to make a profit. It simply existed to serve as a cover platform for his work against the Royal Navy in Bombay. Over the last few months, Steinmark had decided to accumulate some profits to provide needed funds when the time came to leave. Through the informal Abwehr network that linked Steinmark with his colleagues in Brazil and Portugal, he learned in July that the Admiral was arrested and was in prison. Those same colleagues reported that the GESTAPO and the *Sicherheitsdienst* were conducting what was politely called audits of all Abwehr enterprises. His colleague in Rio had already disappeared. Was he in Panama living a new life? Or in the brig on some *Kriegsmarine* cruiser headed back to Germany following one of these audits? Steinmark would never know. What was clear to Steinmark was these audits were purges of the men and women recruited by Canaris — men and women just like him.

Steinmark looked around his office and realized the schizophrenic nature of his current situation. As Major Jan Steinmark, he continued to manage a very successful sabotage operation against the British Navy in Bombay. It didn't matter that the Nazis had arrested his commander. Steinmark felt duty bound to do what he could to accomplish that mission for Germany. On the other hand, as Dom Maximilian Traumann, he was working even harder than usual to expand his profits in both legal business import and export trade and his smuggling operations of Portuguese and Goan goods into British India. Those profits would serve him well when the time came to disappear.

Serving in Goa had its advantages, including life in a tropical paradise in a neutral country. Also, it placed Steinmark half a world away from this Nazi takeover of the German intelligence service. Long before the Nazis decided to "audit" Steinmark's activities, he would be long gone from Goa. The questions that remained were: Where could he go and how much money would he need to get there?

In the past month, he used some of those funds to purchase a larger, ocean worthy sailboat and, with surprisingly little difficulty, a Portuguese passport in a new name. The same skills that made Steinmark a successful Abwehr officer served him well as he prepared to move into the post-war world as a Portuguese mining engineer, most likely in Africa or South America.

While he worked in his office, Steinmark listened to his shortwave radio. Radio Berlin was no longer a choice. He tuned in to the BBC for news or, if he wanted to enjoy music, the American Armed Forces Radio Service. While living in South America in the 1930s, Steinmark had acquired a taste for American jazz music, which the U.S. military radio service seemed to play night and day for their soldiers, sailors and airmen. He was enjoying a bit of jazz, when the music was interrupted by a news broadcast. The American news reader said that a large American and British airborne and armor operation was taking place in Holland with the objective of crossing the Rhine and meanwhile, American forces were on the outskirts of the German city of Aachen. The reader said the invasion of Germany had begun. After that brief news flash, the station returned to the big band jazz music. Steinmark looked at the radio in his darkened office. His plans would have to be accelerated.

T he first debriefing on 16 September had gone as well as could be expected. OSS and SOE debriefers focused on the operations in advance of DRAGOON which they stated had been very successful. German mobility across the entire front had been damaged by their teams and three other Jedburgh teams in the area. At the end of the session, the debriefers focused on the three Resistance groups and O'Connell and his SOE partner Barker offered their shared view that regardless of their politics, Jocelyn's academic communists ended up as the least effective and Henri's crew of farmers and smugglers were the best. Henri's team said they were communists, though it was not clear what the word communist meant to these men.

The French advisor was upset about this assessment simply because Jacques' team of Free French were not listed as the best. He was also murderously angry about what happened to his officer. The Jedburghs went over and over the fact that Broumand was killed by an outsider who had infiltrated Jocelyn's French communist organization. After their linkup with US airborne forces after D-Day for DRAGOON, they had brought Jocelyn into a military police base and subjected her to a less-than-gentle interrogation. The MPs and the Airborne commander, LTC. Edwards, warned the Jedburghs that they would not tolerate a formal arrest because they would have to work with the resistance as the allies defeated the last of the German forces in Southern France.

The interrogation had to be voluntary and Jocelyn was allowed to leave well before either of the surviving Jedburghs were satisfied. What they did get out of her was that the man in the forest was a dock worker from Marseilles, he had fought in the Spanish Civil War and he was a "trusted comrade." They did not tell her he was dead nor did they get an opportunity to confront her about the death of Broumand before she turned to the Airborne commander and asked to leave. Needless to say, the Free French representative in Devonshire did not find this result satisfactory. The Jedburghs agreed. They were convinced that Jocelyn knew more than she was saying. She would be confronted by the French government, eventually, but for now, there was precious little they could do.

On 22 September, O'Connell and Barker returned to the debriefing room to find two well-dressed men in dark suits waiting for them. They introduced themselves as James Angleton, an OSS officer, and Kim Philby, an MI6 officer. They were both from what they called the Twenty Committee in London.

"Twenty committee?" O'Connell was well and truly puzzled.

Barker gave him one of his regular looks like he was speaking to a child. "These gentlemen are from the counterintelligence office in London which goes by the Roman numerals for 20. Peter, you may have heard of them as the Double Cross organization. Get it? Two Xs."

Barker then turned to the two men across the table and said, "Well gentlemen, I don't want to take you away from your evening meal and port at some gentlemen's club in London. Please note. While my friend Major O'Connell has to speak to you because of his OSS affiliation, I am not under any obligation to do so since SOE and MI6 are not necessarily in agreement on who is in charge. Still, if I can help I will do so voluntarily. So, feel free to get this interview started."

The man identified as Angleton started the conversation, "Captain Barker, I wouldn't be so glib if I was you. We are here to determine if you are traitors who killed a Free French officer, who, by the way, actually outranked you and could, perhaps, should have been in charge of your mission."

O'Connell leaned over the table and was about to say something, when Barker placed a right hand on O'Connell's arm and squeezed, hard. While his shoulder wound was healing quickly, reaching over to O'Connell made Barker wince. He said, "Don't mind my friend, gents. After all, we just spent a few weeks in Occupied France. Life on the run and being shot at, and in my case, hit makes you more than a little tired. We are a bit weary of the debriefings."

The MI6 officer took over the conversation, "Excellent. Let's review what you have said about the events from the time Captain Broumand was murdered to the time you described the confrontation with the Frenchman near the canal north of Avignon."

"Let me say again, as I said before in two separate interviews, the creep was a Russian."

"And you assumed that because he used a Russian sniper rifle?"

Barker interjected "And he said he was a Russian."

Angleton took over the conversation. "And we are supposed to believe that is what he said to you? Not a terribly secret agent, was he?"

"He thought Peter was dead and I knew he was trying to get me to talk so he could figure out in the dark where I was. "

"And I come back to the statement, why did you believe him and, for that matter, why should we believe you?"

"Why don't you believe me?"

"Because we think it is awfully convenient, Captain, that you have a dead French officer who was clearly making progress building the Free French resistance in Southern France and now that he is gone, you have just reported that a communist resistance group is the best in the region and recommend we continue to work with them."

Philby looked at Angleton and then over to Barker. At this point, O'Connell began to turn crimson under his tan from months in the countryside in France. Barker tried to continue the conversation in a courteous manner. He knew his partner was ready to explode.

"You really think that is how it happened and why?"

Angleton looked at Barker, "Yes, we are certain that is how and why it happened."

O'Connell stood up. He was not as tall as Angleton but had him by 30 pounds — most of it in his shoulders and arms. He leaned over and looked ready to break the neck of one or both of the interrogators. "So, you are certain, eh?"

Neither officer from XX seemed willing to say something that might inflame an already dangerous situation. O'Connell turned his partner and said, "Certain. These two assholes from London with their perfect suits and custom-made cigarettes and slightly overweight bodies are certain. Perhaps, I should make them less certain, eh?"

O'Connell reached under his shirt.

The two London interrogators jumped up so quickly their chairs tipped onto to the floor with a loud bang. The door opened and two Royal Marine military policemen came in. Both were built like O'Connell with faces that announced they had been in more than one fist fight.

O'Connell slammed his hand on the table and displayed several slightly creased sheets of paper. "This came off the sniper. Displaced person documents in the name of Miroslav Negat, born in Serbia, and a dock workers ID from Marseilles. And, this also came off the sniper, this time sewn inside his black sniper jacket. It is a second document in Cyrillic with a photo of our sniper in a Soviet Major's uniform with the name of Boris Nikolai Beroslav. On the upper right hand corner, there are capital letters which spell SMERSH. I don't know what SMERSH means, heck, I can only sound out the Russian alphabet, but it definitely doesn't mean he was a member of the French Resistance. What do you think about that for certainty? Not good enough? No problem. I will be happy to take you to the grave I dug for this creep near Avignon and you can examine the body more thoroughly. Whatdya say?"

After his speech, O'Connell walked toward the door leaving the papers on the table. The Royal Marines appeared ready to stop him when Philby waved a hand and they parted to let him leave.

Barker stood up, smiled a polite smile and said, "Gentlemen, it has been most interesting. If you don't mind, I think we can safely say that we are done for the day, what? If you want more information, I suggest you reach out to the allied forces in Southern France and pick up Ms. Jocelyn Montreaux, assuming that is her real name."

He walked out and found O'Connell in the corridor trying, unsuccessfully, to light a cigarette with his Zippo lighter. "Just waiting to see if they were going to let you out."

"And when were you going to tell me you had the Russian's documents?"

"I didn't trust any of them and, just as you said before, I barely trusted you. You probably don't know much about poker, but you never show your hand until you bet is called."

"Sounds like gin."

O'Connell put his arm around his fellow Jedburgh and as they walked out the door said, "I think it sounds like a pint."

"After a whiskey."

24 September 1944. OSS Headquarters, London

"I still think he is lying to us. I don't know where he got the documents he offered, but I don't believe either his or Barker's story." James Jesus Angleton had just returned from the debriefing of Peter O'Connell and his British colleague Clive Baker. Angleton was sitting in front of the desk of Lieutenant Colonel Mike Rasmussen. Rasmussen was an OSS/Special Operations officer in England managing all of the OSS/SO operations in France including the mission that O'Connell had just completed. Rasmussen was in his US Marine Corps uniform and Angleton was in a navy blue wool suit covered with cigarette ash. As the counterintelligence chief in the office, Angleton considered himself Rasmussen's superior, though that view was not shared by Rasmussen or by many in OSS/London. That was especially the case since Rasmussen had spent most of 1943 in Yugoslavia hunting and being hunted by Nazis and their Balkan collaborators. He was wearing his OSS jump wings, a Bronze Star and a Purple Heart to prove it.

"And what does your pal Philby think?"

"He doesn't know. The displaced person document O'Connell provided is definitely a forgery — but a very good forgery. It could be German or Soviet or the work of some very good commercial Swiss forger. According to both MI5 and MI6, the Soviet document is real. Whether it is the assassin's document is another question."

"Why don't you take Peter up on his offer and go dig up the body?"

Rasmussen was smiling when he said it. He had read the debriefing report in which O'Connell offered to take Angleton and Philby back to France to dig up the body of the assassin he killed. Rasmussen knew Angleton was not about to go near the front lines, much less disinter a body that had been in a shallow grave for a month. Rasmussen wondered if Angleton even knew what a dead body looked like. He decided to change the subject. "Anyhow, what the heck is SMERSH?"

"According to our British colleagues, it is the enforcement side of Soviet counterintelligence. If you cross paths with SMERSH, it is usually on your way to a bullet in the back of the head."

"Charming, and why doesn't that fit into the debriefing of O'Connell and Barker?"

Angleton could barely remain polite in his response. "It is a good story, a consistent story, but it is too convenient a story. Meanwhile, the French communists are still operating in Southern France with our assistance."

"And why do you have such a hard on for O'Connell? What did he ever do to you?"

"O'Connell may be a good commando, but he could easily have been taken in by the French communists. I don't believe he is loyal."

This time, it was Rasmussen who slammed his hand on the intervening desk. He stood up and leaned over the still teetering oak desk. His large, square head with his fresh Marine haircut and exceptionally close-shaved face was only two inches from Angleton's face when he said, "*Mister* Angleton, I don't know how you measure loyalty, but this is how I measure loyalty. *Major* Peter O'Connell has two combat stars on his jump wings, he has a Bronze star and a Purple Heart from his work in Italy and we are going to recommend him for another Bronze star for this operation in support of DRAGOON. I suspect General Donovan may boost the award up to a Silver Star given the level of success, the risks taken, and the hardship faced by JEDBURGH CRANKCASE. O'Connell's SOE pal Captain Barker has already been promoted and recommended for the Military Cross. By the way, your pal Philby has already cleared Barker for reassignment to the CBI theater and supported the award."

Rasmussen lowered his voice but did not sit down. He continued, "Now, *Mister* Angleton, if you want to question this man's loyalty, I recommend you leave my office now and go down to the head, wash your hands, and then look into the mirror. YOU need to decide how you define loyalty and consider what loyalty means in combat. Then, just for your own sake, think about how much discussion of this incident might affect your own assignment here. Or, for that matter, any future assignments you might have with the OSS or with any other intelligence organization in the US government. Think about that very carefully when you complete your final report for the old man." Angleton was not a physical man. He was surprised every time OSS/SO and even OSS/Secret Intelligence operators threatened him for offering his views based on information and what he saw as the obvious, logical conclusions. He knew the enemy was organized and focused on turning OSS representatives to support their operations. He had seen how successful XX Committee was in turning German representatives and how that had been confirmed by the team at Bletchley Park Signals Intelligence. This was information that he was certain Rasmussen didn't even know and would never understand. The covert world of espionage was complex, and counterespionage was all about looking for complexity when the "reality" appeared to be too simple. He rarely was interested just in "facts," he was interested in "truth."

His British colleagues, and most especially Philby, had been very thorough in their efforts to explain to him the nature of treason and how easy it had been for the Germans to use right wing parties in England and France before the war for their own ends. Angleton knew that the Soviets were equally good and equally determined. He knew from Philby that people like O'Connell and Rasmussen who came from families of laborers and union members were their primary targets. There was even some information from Philby, courtesy of the British Security Service, that O'Connell's extended family might include a member of the Irish Republican Army. Angleton knew that, unlike himself and his British MI6 colleagues, who were well educated and from the elite of society, workers, unionists and their children were easily sold on Soviet propaganda. Rasmussen might be a decent Marine officer, but Angleton doubted his intellectual credentials. Operations by both the Nazis and the Soviets would be carefully designed and would be protected by "facts." It was up to the experts like Angleton to understand the underlying truth that was revealed by the wealth of facts.

He stood up, buttoned his three-button Savile Row suit and left the room without responding in any way to Rasmussen's challenge. He returned to his office and began to type up his assessment of Jedburgh CRANKCASE and why he recommended that O'Connell and Barker be detained and interrogated in the MI5 facility near Dartmoor prison. He suspected his MI5 colleagues would be sympathetic. O'Connell was Irish after all and MI5 were always interested in Irish sympathizers to the German cause.

After Angleton departed, Rasmussen left his office, climbed the stairs and walked into the office of the London chief of OSS/ Secret Intelligence. The occupant was sitting behind another old oak desk, wearing his US Navy lieutenant's uniform. "Bill, I know you have more than enough on your plate right now, but I also know you are close to the old man and I need some help right now."

Bill Casey looked up from his desk. Regardless of the difference in ranks, he and Rasmussen were close, sharing books, drinks and games of chess. Casey liked the SO chief for his candor and his dedication to his men in the field. Even the natural jealousies between a career Marine officer and Casey, as an officer in the Naval Reserve, were tempered with wise cracks. Unlike most in the office, Casey also knew that Rasmussen had a law degree from Dartmouth and worked for the US Navy Office of the Solicitor and Judge Advocate General before the war. Rasmussen's legal credentials resulted in Donovan reaching out to him in 1942. Casey said, "I suspect this has to do with Angleton, right?"

"You heard?"

"Who hasn't? For an outfit that's supposed to keep secrets, the gossip in 70 Grosvenor is worse than any I ever saw in the civilian world. What do you want from me?"

"I just need someone outside my office to understand that Angleton is barking up the wrong tree right now and, to keep the analogy going, he is like a dog with a bone. He is not going to let this one go. O'Connell is a full-fledged hero. The Brits think so. I think so, and I know the boss is going to think so. I don't want Angleton pissing on his parade because he doesn't like combat heroes or because he doesn't like Irishmen. Neither of those arguments will go over too well with the General. Still, I don't want this bullshit to reach him if I can help it. What do we do?"

Casey looked at his coffee cup and then up at Rasmussen. "Here is what I recommend. James is about to be reassigned to Rome anyhow, so he will be out of here in a month. During that reassignment process, his report on O'Connell just might get mislaid and then, by accident, destroyed. I think it is entirely likely that an accident like that will happen." Casey underscored this by pointing to his in-box.

"Meanwhile, we can reassign O'Connell to the China, Burma, India Theatre, possibly OSS/SO Detachment 101, but anyplace in that theatre. I understand SOE has done the same with Barker. That way, we immediately get him out of the gunsight of Angleton and the clutches of any of the little Angletonians that James Jesus might have fostered here in London. O'Connell is a good operator, but I also think the Free French are not going to let this one go anytime soon. CBI is much more of a US-UK show and that means he will be able to succeed and probably thrive out there."

Rasmussen had played chess with Casey enough to know that nothing was ever what it seemed with his friend. "And you might have something you want done in the CBI?"

"Funny you should say that, Mike. I happen to have a target in India that I want to go after. He is an undercover German intelligence agent. I know our CI folks, including Angleton, don't think the German Abwehr works out in the CBI, but I have tracked him there based on a file that Dulles in Bern got from his sources in the Abwehr. This target is out on a very long end of the rope. Once Canaris was arrested, we can assume many of the Abwehr field agents have wondered how long it will be before the GESTAPO comes knocking on their door. You know what Operation FAUST is about and how successful Dulles has been in focusing on operations in Germany proper. FAUST is all about penetrating Germany and doing it now. The German Army is retreating, but that doesn't mean it is finished. We need all the information we can get from any source we can."

Casey continued, "So, if O'Connell just happened to stop in Bombay for a bit of time on his way to meet with his future OSS Detachment commander in Calcutta, well, it might be possible for him to find and possibly recruit a certain Abwehr Major Jan Steinmark, German paratrooper, Knight's Cross with Oakleaves. Steinmark was in German special operations in North Africa. He was wounded there and lost an eye. He is now located in the neutral Portuguese colony of Goa. O'Connell might see if he would like to change sides. Three years under cover as a Brazilian businessman has to be pretty hard on the psyche. Maybe a fellow paratrooper might be better at gaining some trust than the British Colonial Intelligence agents."

"So, you can make this happen?"

"I already started the paperwork yesterday. I was just waiting for Angleton to piss you off enough to come see me."

>>>>>> **DILETTANTE**

10-12 October 1944 — London to Bombay, India

The interior of the B24 was cold and dark. This particular B24 had served the Carpetbaggers out of England for the last two years. Their long-range night flights into occupied Europe delivered OSS individuals, teams, or supplies keeping the resistance alive. Now, this crew was traveling to India to do the same mission in the China, Burma and India (CBI) Theatre. O'Connell was strapped into one of the few web seats in the aircraft — sitting next to the navigator and the flight engineer. He had no on-board duties, so he shoved cotton in his ears and tried to rest. Even wearing coveralls over his uniform and his leather flight jacket over that, he was cold. So far, he hadn't had much luck resting as the aircraft hopped from England to Libya, Libya to Aden, Aden to Basra and now the leg from Basra to Bombay. After that, the crew would fly on to Calcutta to support the OSS detachments based in South East Asia. At each stop, the aircraft dropped off some cargo for the OSS contingent in the area. He helped the crew off-load the boxes and bags and, in rare occasions, take on locked bags headed to the CBI headquarters in Kandy, Ceylon.

O'Connell remained furious with his own outfit, or at least one member of his outfit, who had accused him of treason after the last mission. What made it worse in his mind was that he viewed the accuser as a limp-wristed, London based guy who smoked hand-crafted cigarettes and wore a Savile Row suit covered with cigarette ash. The guy seemed to be trying to be more British than the British. His Brit partner was more polite but just as snooty. Neither of them had been anywhere close to the front lines and their understanding of resistance groups was based only on what they had read, not what they had seen or done. His Italian partners claimed to be communists but didn't know anything about what the term meant. In France, one of the teams made up of academics understood communist dogma but could barely accomplish simple sabotage missions. It really wasn't until he met the SMERSH assassin that O'Connell understood that the Soviets were determined to turn those "communists" into surrogates for some future control of Europe.

Even on the flight to the other side of the world, he was unable to quiet the raging anger in his mind. These "experts" sat in the safety of London while trying to judge him for his actions behind enemy lines. Didn't they know the war was against the Nazis and the Japs not against their own soldiers? The only reason he didn't hunt down the two creeps and choke them after they had brandy and soda and left some London club was the intercession of his British colleague Clive Barker. Life in the OSS was complicated enough without internal rivalries. Later, he had a discussion about this with his OSS/Special Operations commander, Major Rasmussen, who had spent 1943 behind the lines. The major told O'Connell not to worry. He would solve the problem in London, but O'Connell needed to, as the major said, get out of the kill zone.

So, Rasmussen cut orders for O'Connell's reassignment to the CBI first to support an OSS mission in Bombay and, then, take the first available flight to Calcutta and to meet with the Detachment 404 commander. Det 404 was responsible for OSS/SO missions in Burma and French Indo-China and he would be assigned to one of those missions "for the duration." The major said, "By the time the war is over, no one is going to give a hoot what the CI shitbirds thought about your work in France or about the communists in the resistance. Hell, O'Connell. You worked in Italy with communists and I worked with Tito's communists in Yugoslavia. Do you think anyone cares? All your record is going to say is that you were killing Nazis."

When O'Connell asked him how that would happen, the major smiled and said, "Because I am going to be the one writing the history of our support to DRAGOON. For now, your job is to stay alive in the jungle paradise of the CBI. Get going."

A slight, but rapid drop in altitude brought O'Connell back to the present. Next to him was his B4 bag holding a two tropical-weight class B uniforms, two sets of what he was told were "jungle fatigues" in some sort of green and brown pebble pattern, his DOP shaving kit, three sets of underwear and socks. He also had a couple of books, including some written by Rudyard Kipling since O'Connell heard he wrote about India. He had purchased most of his kit in London since his field gear from France was too dirty, too torn and too hot for the CBI. The only thing he kept was his leather jacket. Too many miles and memories to throw away.

It was cold in the aircraft, but he knew that even in the winter, India had a tropical climate. It was bad enough he wasn't sure why he was going to India, but he had no desire he to work someplace where the temperatures stayed well about 100 degrees in the summer and there were snakes. O'Connell hated snakes. Navy Lieutenant Casey, the London boss of OSS Secret Intelligence, had told him was he needed to get to Bombay and report to the OSS unit commander. He would be briefed when he got there. During his training, he heard about Detachment 101 working in the jungles of Burma building teams of tribesmen to fight the Japanese and he knew Det 404 was going to do the same in French Indo-China. In London, he heard of new teams leaving Calcutta headed in all directions in Asia including China, Siam and Indo-China. The interim stop in Bombay remained a puzzle. It made no sense to him, but O'Connell had grown used to OSS ways over the last year. Sometimes the lack of information was because of security and need to know. Sometimes it was because OSS was a real scatter-shot organization where doctrine, bureaucracy and, heaven forbid, chain of command rarely affected the mission.

By the time the aircraft approached Bombay over the Arabian Sea, the interior had shifted from cold through cool to warm to hot. O'Connell was certain that when they landed, they would immediately be baked in the heat. The flight engineer came up to O'Connell and shouted over the engine noise, "Major, we aren't going to stay on the ground long. Our station is in Calcutta and right now the Bombay airport is listing the ground temperature at close to 100 degrees. The monsoon season is late this year and that means it never cooled off from the summer heat. If it gets too much warmer, we aren't going to be able to take off. Skipper says he has no intention of spending the night in Bombay so he isn't even going to shut down the engines. We have enough fuel to get to Calcutta and he intends to do so. What I'm saying is that when the aircraft lands, we want you off our airplane."

"Fair enough, Jesse. All I have is my B4 bag so as soon as you open the hatch, I'll be gone from your life."

"Don't count on never seeing us again, Major. We all know you are with SO from the SF wings on your right shoulder and SO is what we support. I suspect we will put you out that Joe Hole sooner or later and probably over some crummy jungle in Burma. Anyhow, best of luck in India. You have anyone picking you up on the flight line?"

"Beats me."

"One recommendation for you: Take off the flight jacket now and store it in the B4 bag. You ain't gonna need it at 100 degrees."

"Good idea, Jesse." O'Connell pulled off his jacket and stuffed it into the large exterior pocket of the B4. Before he zipped up the pocket, he pulled out his overseas cap with his new major's oak leaf rank and on the opposite side, the glider patch. The coveralls had no rank and he wasn't about to completely undress.

The landing was smooth and as soon as they reached the end of the runway, the aircraft spun 180 degrees and lined up for takeoff. The flight engineer walked back, cracked the crew access door and dropped the stairs. The air felt like an oven and the reflected heat from the tarmac was even worse. The smells of Bombay hit O'Connell like a slap in the face. Aviation fuel, smoke, sea and sewage. Jesse shook O'Connell's hand and said, "See you soon, Major. Keep cool."

Before O'Connell could turn and wave, the flight engineer had closed the crew door and the aircraft was rolling down the runway. O'Connell moved quickly out of the way as the twin tail of the B24 raced past him. He squinted in the haze and late afternoon sun looking for something that might serve as an aircraft terminal or, if not that, at least some shade. He reached into a pocket in the coveralls and pulled out a pair of green lens sunglasses from the UK military stores in London. He hadn't expected to need the sunglasses, but in the tropical heat, he realized without them he would be blind from the sun. As soon as he put them on, O'Connell saw an Army jeep racing toward him, initially indistinct in the heat waves, but eventually becoming more and more clear. O'Connell was pleased to see that the jeep had the top canvas on. It would offer a little shade. The jeep halted with a squeak of the brakes.

"You O'Connell?

"Yes."

"I'm Standish. Number two here in this hellhole. Get in before you melt into the tarmac."

O'Connell threw his bag in the back and jumped in. The jeep took off before his right foot had left the tarmac. Over his shoulder, O'Connell could see the B24 banking to the East heading to Calcutta.

Standish shouted as the jeep ran down the length of the runway. "Gotta drive fast or you boil here. "

"I would have thought you might bake."

"In Bombay, you boil, or have the rubber tires stick to the tarmac." Standish grinned. He was dressed in short sleeve tropical uniform blouse, shorts, brown field boots and a hat that was officially called "helmet, sun, rigid, fiber" and looked to O'Connell like something out of a movie about African safaris. He was wearing a .45 on his right hip and a Colt Commando .38 in a military issue, sweat soaked leather shoulder holster.

"Two guns?"

"Heck, O'Connell, you never know around here. The Brit civilian and military police hate it when we wear our weapons, so just to be amusing, I wear two. That makes them hate me twice as much and that's just fine by me. What you won't hear from our British colleagues is there is an active Indian resistance movement supported by the Japs. Mostly on the other side of the country, but periodically, some knucklehead throws a grenade in a military vehicle here in Bombay or sabotages some facility at the Navy Yard. They are convinced by the Japs that they will be free if the Japs win out here. What crap! Anyhow, I figure if I see someone getting ready to send a pineapple my way while driving this jeep, it will be easier to use the .38 to cap him before he pulls the pin. You got a gun, O'Connell?"

"Yup. A .45 under the flight suit."

"OK, just sayin' you might be prepared to use it." Standish shifted again, let out the clutch on the jeep and accelerated. "Welcome to the Raj."

Based on his previous map study, O'Connell expected the drive from the airfield to the OSS office in Bombay would be an hour's journey. O'Connell had heard about the chaos of British India traffic, but he wasn't prepared for the mix of military trucks, taxis, horse drawn taxis called tongas, horse drawn wagons and crowds of pedestrians and beggars all sharing the road. Somehow, with Standish's offensive driving skills, they made the trip in forty five minutes. Standish instructed O'Connell to use the small hand cranked siren on the side of the jeep at key intersections so that some, though not all of the traffic parted for them to pass. Eventually, they arrived at a walled bungalow on Malabar Hill overlooking what was known as the "Queen's Necklace" road linking the British civilian government buildings to the Royal Navy Yard.

As they rolled into the compound and the local guards closed and bolted the gate, O'Connell was greeted by a thin, balding man dressed in local garb of white cotton pants and a white, long cotton shirt that reached to his knees. He wore a white straw hat, round green tinted sunglasses and was smoking a cigarette mounted in an ivory cigarette holder.

"Peter, welcome to India. Come in and take tea!"

Standish leaned over to O'Connell and said, "That's our boss,

Navy Commander Patrick Donohue. He was a trader here before the war, at least that what he says. For sure a Navy officer during the last war. Good guy, knows his stuff. Reserve commission like most of us, so he's not a real stickler on regulations, either Army or Navy. A little eccentric, but he gets the job done and gives me plenty of work, so I'm not about to complain…much." Standish nodded toward the chief and then over to the left of the jeep. "Get out, go have tea with the boss and I'll stow your kit in your bungalow over there against the wall."

"Standish, do you know why I'm here?"

"I saw your orders. You are working in this madhouse on some special project against Nazis. We don't have any of them here, so I guess it is going to be a challenge."

O'Connell went inside the main house as Standish drove the jeep around to the back. The transition from bright sunlight to the dark interior of the house was dramatic as was the transition from heat to cool air. Donohue watched O'Connell's face as he slowly wandered into the entryway of the bungalow.

"Always good to see the reaction. Amazing what good architecture can do in the proper environment, eh? My first trip to the region was in 1932. I arrived by steamer and landed in Bombay harbor. Thought my head would explode from the heat and then I checked into the Taj Hotel, walked into the Sea Lounge Bar and suddenly the heat vanished, and I was sold on the subcontinent. I hope you are starting to realize that it is not all heat and masses of humanity. At least, not for now."

"Sir, thanks for the initiation into the Raj. Did you say take tea?"

"Yes, my son. We take tea here in the Raj. You need to keep hydrated here and it is too soon for cocktails and I don't want to expose you to too many diseases on your first day. So, tea made with heavily boiled water and milk." Donohue turned to a shadow O'Connell could see deeper in the bungalow and said, "Mohammed, we will be on the veranda."

"Yes, sir." The shadow disappeared into the deeper confines of the house.

"Follow me, Peter. I promise we will just take a bit of tea and then you can get washed up and changed and we can talk shop. By the way, my colleague Mohammed Mahsud is not a servant, he is part of the team. He has been with me for nearly a decade. We were mates in the rubber industry and now he is willing to keep me healthy here in Bombay. You need to know, I trust him completely, probably more than I trust you."

As the strangeness of this introduction to the subcontinent continued to wash over him, all Peter could do was nod.

After a cup of sweet, milky tea, another of Donohue's house staff lead O'Connell to his "quarters" in the far end of the compound. His bungalow included a large sitting room, a bedroom and a separate bathroom. There was a bath drawn with lukewarm water. O'Connell's clothes including his leather flight jacket were already moved from the B4 bag into the closet. On the bed was a new tropical uniform including underwear, short sleeved shirt, shorts, long socks. At the foot of the bed were a new pair of rough out boots with crepe soles. O'Connell took off his field boots, stripped off the flight coverall, took off his shoulder holster and pistol, dropped his underwear in the pile and jumped into the bath.

Days of aircraft travel left behind and freshly shaved, he reentered the bedroom to find the green coverall and underwear gone and the leather shoulder holster, freshly rubbed with saddle oil, hanging in the closet. His .45 and his two spare magazines were treated with gun oil, wiped down and resting on a new canvas pistol belt and holster. He noticed that a new set of major's oak leaves were on the collars of his uniform as well as a new set of ribbons including his European theatre ribbon, purple heart, and Bronze star with V device.

"It is magic," O'Connell said to no one in particular as he dressed in the clean cotton uniform, moving his pistol in its new canvas-holster home into a drawer in the writing desk on the far side of the room. He walked back toward the main compound across the freshly mowed lawn and what appeared to be a full-sized croquet court.

He found Donohue and Standish on the veranda working on another pot of tea. This time the table was laid with plates and silverware, a pitcher of lemonade, a large pile of sandwiches, and fresh cut fruit.

"Peter, you look so much better. Did the uniform fit? We had to guess based on the picture in your personnel file and the assumption that you lost a little weight in France."

"Sir, it fits perfectly. Thanks."

"Great. By the way, amongst us kids, I'm Patrick," Donohue pointed to Standish, "And he's Michael."

"But we do call him Sir when the Brits are around so that we maintain some semblance of military discipline, mostly just to fool them," Standish said. "He is Navy after all."

O'Connell filled a plate from the tray, poured a glass of lemonade, and sat down. "Michael, I think we are going to get along just fine, though I have a far better opinion of the Brits than you do. My SOE partner in France was good people."

Donohue interceded, "I think Michael is just tired of being lectured by both India Special Branch and British security service personnel. My work with SOE has also been most satisfactory. Early in the war, I also did a turn with the Royal Marines in Rangoon before it fell. Good fellows all."

Midway through a sandwich, Standish said, "Patrick, you just need to send me out to Burma with the SOE and I will change my view, I promise."

"It's only a matter of time, my boy. But first, we need to accomplish some things in Goa and that is where Peter enters the equation."

O'Connell was tired of being kept in the dark and said, "Patrick, I'm confused and a bit annoyed that I'm the only one in the room who doesn't know what I'm supposed to do here."

"On the table, son. Your operational file is on the table along with your tea. Michael, you should continue to eat and not interrupt Peter until he has had some food and read the file. Understand?"

"Patrick, I will do my best."

O'Connell decided to read while eating. Possibly not the best choice for either digestion or understanding, but he simply couldn't wait. He opened up the brown file labeled DILETTANTE. On the internal flap of the file were two pictures of the same man. One in German paratrooper battle uniform and another in a dark suit. In the second picture, the man had a deep scar from his forehead to his jaw. O'Connell flipped the page and started read the three type written pages.

Target DILETTANTE: German Intelligence (Abwehr) Major Jan Steinmark operating in the Portuguese colony of Goa.

Description: Steinmark arrived in Goa ca. Christmas of 1942 under the alias name Maximilian Traumann, a Brazilian citizen with business ties to Portugal and Spain. His cover business, MERCURY CORPORACAO, focuses on light industry shipments to Goa, specifically small electrical generators used by the Portuguese colonial administrators and port officials and Goan fruits and vegetables shipped back to Portugal. His cover job allows him to maintain good contacts with Portuguese officials and to make regular trips both to the port and periodic trips in customs boats to Portuguese and Spanish flagged ships anchored off the coast of Goa waiting for a port berth.

Biographic information: Steinmark was born in Potsdam in 1892 into a family of Prussian officers. We are not certain if he served in any military capacity during the Great War. He graduated from the University of Heidelberg in 1923 with a degree in engineering. Steinmark traveled to Chile, Argentina and Brazil from 1925 to 1933 working for German oil exploration and development companies. American business contacts from that time report Steinmark fluent in Portuguese, Spanish, and Italian. He speaks what they described as "reasonable" English. In 1933, he returned to Germany and joined the Weimar Republic's German Reichswehr as a cavalry officer and remained in the cavalry when the Nazi's voided the Versailles Treaty and created the German Wehrmacht. Source: Office of Naval Intelligence reporting.

War Service: Steinmark's military record shows that he served on the Eastern Front. More recent source reporting has Steinmark serving in North Africa from 1940 to 1941 as an officer in Abwehr supervising special operations in a unit known as the Brandenburg Division. He was wounded in 1941. He lost an eye during a deep raid against British forces in Palestine. He returned to Berlin for recuperation and received the Knight's Cross with oak leaves for his service in North Africa. He was transferred to Abwehr Headquarters under unknown circumstances. We believe he has some personal connections to Abwehr chief, Admiral Canaris. We do not know if he is a loyal Nazi. Given his affiliation with the Abwehr, we believe there is a chance that he was more loyal to Canaris than to the Nazi party. Since Canaris' arrest, we have no information on how that has affected any Abwehr operations other than the bureaucratic transfer of Abwehr operations to the Reich Main Security Office which is part of the Sicherheitsdienst (SD), the intelligence arm of the Schutzstaffel (SS). Source: OSS Bern.

Mission: Recruit and/or disrupt Steinmark using whatever means necessary to gain access to the German network operating in Goa and India. Acquire Steinmark's communications system and his code books. Obtain as much information as possible on the current situation in Berlin and how it affects the Abwehr agents in the field.

Additional security measures: Our agreements with our British allies prevent any official operation of this type. India and Goa are considered a primary area of responsibility of Britain and most especially the Government of India Special Branch. The Government of India reluctantly supports SOE bases in India; they are hostile to our efforts across the region. Therefore, your cover for the mission is you are working to set up additional training capability for the Burma operations of Detachment 101 in Burma through Detachment 303 in New Delhi. Your time in Bombay is not official and your infiltration into Goa will not be revealed to the British government.

Once Peter looked up from the file and lunch was cleared from the table, Donohue and Standish provided additional information. Standish opened the conversation, "Peter, you have accomplished your first step in the mission by arriving in Bombay without incident. Well done."

"Michael, your observation skills remain unmatched," Donohue offered in a less than supportive tone. "Peter, we have all read the report and have our own views of the job. Before we offer our perspective, I wanted to hear what you think."

O'Connell was still digesting both his lunch and the file and not yet on the right time zone. He was having trouble staying awake much less focusing on the operation, but he realized that he had to say something. "I think the best plan is to conduct a raid on Steinmark's house, kill him and steal whatever materials he has. It seems the simplest way to shut down the Nazi operation and acquire his codes." It was not exactly a refined view of the mission, but one that was consistent with OSS methods he had used in Italy and France.

Donohue looked across the table at Standish, "Well?"

"I'm all for Peter's recommendation. Steinmark is on his own, right? How hard is it going to be to break into a house in Goa and do the job?"

Donohue looked at the two younger men and sighed. "I guess we have a consensus from the action men at the table. Perhaps that is why headquarters sent me killers instead of spies."

O'Connell raised his hands in mock surrender and said, "Patrick, I just read the file, so don't expect a sophisticated answer until I've had more tea and more time!"

"Fair enough, young O'Connell. Let me offer a couple of thoughts on the project. First, the file is very clear we don't know very much about Steinmark. Is he a Nazi or just a loyal German soldier trying to do his job? What precisely was his job when he first arrived? We do not know. What is his current mission? We do not know."

Donohue paused over his tea and said, "So, what type of network was here when he got here and what missions did *they* have? If he did have a personal relationship with Canaris as the file suggests, how loyal do you think he is today after he found out this summer that Canaris was arrested by the Nazis? How much access do you think he has to the Abwehr or to efforts in Berlin to combine military intelligence with the Nazi party security services? Before we decide to mount a commando raid on a bungalow in Goa, I think we might want to collect a bit more information. We might even be able to recruit Steinmark and have him work against the Nazis for a longer period than you suggested. The war isn't over yet, men. I think a longer-term recruitment might be better than a short-term smash and grab. That's what I am thinking."

Standish looked over at O'Connell. "That's why I'm still here and not in Burma. He keeps trying to reform me after my time in Yugoslavia."

"And I suspect that is why the OSS headquarters keeps sending commandos to learn how to do more than run bandits in the mountains." Donohue was smiling as he said that, but O'Connell noted that Donohue's eyes were not part of the smile. Donohue was serious and if there was anything that O'Connell had learned from his military service, it was that if his commander was serious then he needed to pay attention.

"So, here is what I recommend," Donohue looked at O'Connell. "Before you collapse from lack of sleep, you need to get out on the street with Michael and see a bit of Bombay. The only way you are going to defeat the fact that your body thinks you are still on some European time zone is to get some sun on your face. You need to understand where you are going to work and some of the limitations you have here. When you get back, I will have a cold dinner delivered to the bungalow and then I want you to get at least eight hours of sleep. Tomorrow we will sit down and get serious about this project. I have received notice from Delhi and London. This is the most important OSS/SI project in the CBI. Needless to say, we all have to put on our thinking caps and consider the possibilities."

Donohue turned to Standish and said, "Change into civilian clothes, take the Buick and drive Peter around. Try not to cause any trouble. Get him back here before dark. Clear?"

Standish was already on his feet. "Yes, sir. Peter, let's get you into civvies that we bought for you and get out on the street. It will be nasty hot, but that's what the boss wants and that's what you are going to get."

12 October 1944. Panjim Harbor, Portuguese colony of Goa

Steinmark was sitting in his home overlooking the harbor, watching the sun go down as he smoked his thirtieth Turkish cigarette of the day. On the table were a properly chilled bottle of local Portuguese white wine, a glass, a loaf of bread, and a local cheese on a plate under a glass dome. Even after all his time in Goa, he was uncomfortable with the heat. Since the cooling monsoon was late, he found himself particularly irritable, as were many Goans and certainly all the Europeans in the colony.

His most recent orders from Berlin had not improved his temper and he had been sitting at the table for nearly an hour trying to determine how he was going to accomplish his new assignment. For the first time in his military career, he was even considering whether he intended to follow orders.

It was clearly a sign of the times that his orders were very limited in scope and precise in direction. When Canaris was in charge, Abwehr commands were delivered more as suggestions than instructions. This allowed him to accomplish whatever he could on his own initiative. Under Schellenberg, this was no longer the case. Steinmark received direct orders, and each encrypted message ended with a warning of the penalties of failure. Steinmark was a soldier and he needed none of this to motivate him. What was disturbing was the nature of the new mission. It was something he had hoped he would never see. Something was seriously amiss in Berlin. Schellenberg's instructions required him to support an exfiltration mechanism for Nazi leadership and Nazi wealth. What was equally disturbing was who he would be working with and what he was expected to trade for the exfiltration.

Steinmark was used to creating his own networks and creating his own luck. Now, he would be relying on someone else's network and, worse still, it would be an enemy network. The war reporting he was hearing on the BBC from his short wave radio must be far closer to the truth than the newspapers coming from Lisbon or Madrid. He looked at the Italian watch on his left wrist. His sister gave it to him when he graduated from the Brandenburg training program. Her husband had purchased it for him while working with a group of Italian rocket engineers. It was supposed to be the watch used by the most elite of the Italian Navy divers known as Decima Flottiglia MAS. It was certainly a survivor. The watch had been with him throughout his time as a commando leader in the Brandenburger Division and it was the only item that survived that night on the Palestinian beach. More recently, he used it on small boat operations up the Indian coast as he set up his sabotage network. He saw it as a good luck talisman if there ever was one. And, with the new orders, he would require more than a bit of good fortune to survive.

Steinmark shook his head, working to force his mind back to the immediate issue. It was time to return to the life of the Brazilian trader and social butterfly, Maximilian Traumann. He was to be the guest of the harbor master tonight and, with luck, he would see the Irish businesswoman who frequented the harbor master's dinners. Later, he would visit the local casino and lose just enough to make everyone involved happy, including the local gangsters who ran the casino. On this night, it was an act that would require supreme focus. The new orders meant that the Nazi Party had decided that the war was lost. The sacrifices made by Steinmark and so many others had been for nothing. The orders also meant it was time for Steinmark to begin to implement his own survival plan.

He took a last sip from the wine glass and focused his attention on the evening ahead. As a first step, Steinmark reached into the desk drawer on the right side of his desk and withdrew a small jewel box. It held his glass eye and a gold Omega watch on a fine tooled leather strap. No eyepatches or military watches for the locals. He then pulled out a second, locked box from the drawer which had his compact Mauser 7.65mm pistol and a glove leather shoulder holster. It was hardly the manstopper of the Luger he kept at the warehouse, but it was easily concealed. While he never expected trouble in Goa, he also knew that trouble often visited those who went unprepared. Steinmark might be many things, but he would not be one of the unprepared. He went into his bedroom to undress, bathe and change for the evening.

For the first week in India, Peter O'Connell got up before dawn each day and went out into the courtyard. While the gardens were hardly an exercise yard, Standish had crafted a chin-up bar and an inclined bench for exercises. After a brief warmup, he and Standish left the compound for a run in the neighborhood. Regardless of when they left, they always passed Donohue and Mohammed on their return from a morning "quick time" walk. The first time they passed Donohue and Mohammed, Standish told O'Connell that he tried to keep up with them on one of these walks and found that after the first hour, he had to turn back before he collapsed. Both Donohue and Mohammed carried a leather shoulder bag with binoculars, a book on bird identification for India, and a notebook. Whether it was for cover or Donohue really was an amateur naturalist, Standish could not say. He suspected Donohue's bag also carried a pistol and Mohammed's either a pistol or a knife. Neither Standish nor O'Connell ever asked, and Donohue never said.

After breakfast each morning, the three OSS officers focused their attention on DILETTANTE. Donohue described parts of his established network in Goa and provided reports from his sources. He explained that while Europeans made great distinctions on the border between British India and Portuguese Goa, the locals saw no reason to follow some line on a map. That was especially the case with the small Indian Christian community in Bombay. Their relatives were in Goa and they often spent holidays there. Once Donohue received the instructions for the DILETTANTE operation, he expanded his efforts with that community to better understand Goa and, more important, their target: Steinmark aka Traumann.

Once O'Connell was fully recovered from his travel, Donohue took the opportunity to teach his two junior officers a bit about tradecraft beyond what they had received in the abbreviated course at the OSS training facility in Maryland. First, he underscored that he always used some sort of cover to work "in plain sight." His early morning exercise routine linked to his birdwatching made a perfect cover. "After all, birds are like people here. They are out early in the morning and out late at night. They are never active in the heat of the day. So, we go out when birds go out and we go to where other birdwatchers go. There is nothing about our walks to arouse suspicion."

O'Connell thought through Donohue's comments and asked, "But if you go where others go and then return, how do you meet your sources?"

"Peter, our meetings are brief, and our contacts have their own cover. Mohammed and I are often accosted by beggars on the street. He works hard to sweep them aside and sometimes we give them a small pittance because, after all, both Christians and Muslims believe in charity. But our beggars are actually literate, well paid informants. They know how to look and act like beggars. During those brief moments, Mohammed passes out requirements and receives written reports."

Donohue stopped to light a cigarette and continued, "Gentlemen, these local sources are essential to collection because Europeans never see their Indian laborers or servants as a threat. They treat them as if they were invisible. Mohammed taught me that, years ago."

Standish added quietly, "Which is one of the reasons the Japanese have sources here."

Donohue heard the comment and countered, "And why some of the more sophisticated members of the Government of India Special Branch have local sources as well. It is why we take good care to vet our staff. You may have noticed that our staff are all Muslims. What you could not have known is they are all Mohammed's relatives."

With each set of reports, a clearer picture emerged of Steinmark's business and daily routine. Steinmark was an established figure both on the docks of Vasco de Gama and Panjim harbors and the government and businessmen's houses in Panjim. As Donohue said, "he lives his cover as a Brazilian trader."

Steinmark appeared to take personal interest in his trade goods. He could be seen checking the goods on delivery to his warehouses and as they left the warehouse headed to local shops. He was active in multiple social clubs in the city, playing cards with Colonial administrators, riding horses with the chief of police, sailing with wealthy Portuguese businessmen in Goa and attending Mass every Sunday where he was one of the most important donors to the restoration of the Cathedral de Santa Catalina. The reporting from Donohue's Christian Goan intelligence network made it very clear that Steinmark committed himself to becoming a pillar of the community. The only unexplained pattern was that the "trader" and a small crew left Panjim harbor the third Wednesday of the month on a nicely outfitted sailing yacht. They always returned on Friday before dark. Some locals said he liked to sail and some people said he liked to fish. No one really knew why he left or precisely when he returned. Donohue said, "Remember what I said about working in plain sight. This is how Steinmark meets his network. The Arabian Sea is large and the Indian coast has many coves. I doubt we are going to sort out where he is goes or who he sees unless we ask him."

All three men agreed that if they didn't have the file in front of them that said Steinmark aka Traumann was a German spy, they would have had little in the way of evidence that this was the case.

"I don't know where a man with his military background learned to be such a good intelligence officer, but he is absolutely good at what he does," Donahue concluded. "He is going to be tough to get next to and tougher still to disrupt without running a chance of a few months if not years in a Goa prison. While the Portuguese colonial administration remains neutral, they would be more than willing to detain American miscreants threatening one of their most important residents."

And it was this challenge that began to capture their attention. Steinmark was a public figure, so meeting him wouldn't be hard. What would be hard would be meeting him in a way that wouldn't end up with a long prison sentence. Donohue added, "Our British colleagues also recognize Goa is a center for espionage and, perhaps, sabotage, against the Empire. They have reduced the number of border crossings and made sea travel between India and Goa difficult. The Portuguese authorities responded by making it just as hard for foreigners to travel to Goa."

"Take a note, my young friends: Espionage is never easy when borders are closed. The British should have avoided this sort of tension and their own Special Branch would have been far better served. With relatively open borders, they would have been able to run their sources and watch for infiltration at the normal crossings. Instead, they have to watch for clandestine infiltration along the entire coast and their own sources face the same challenge in Goa. How annoying for us, no?"

After two weeks of collection and planning, they spent another afternoon running multiple scenarios that offered little chance of success. Their new information had been limited to the agent collection Donohue recovered every third or fourth day from Goa. They knew more about MERCURY CORPORACOA business and some about Steinmark's day to day activities, but they still hadn't figured out how they were going to infiltrate O'Connell and Standish into the Portuguese colony for the close reconnaissance and assessment of their target.

After a particularly frustrating morning, Donohue abruptly stood up from the table in the study and said, "Gentlemen, I have decided to solve our problem of how to get into Goa. I will be back in two hours." Standish and O'Connell looked at each other as Donohue walked out of the room. They heard him shout into another part of the house, "Mohammed, *sanga yeh!*" In seconds, Mohammed was at Donohue's side with their two shoulder bags and they were out the door.

"What did he say?"

"Peter, I have no idea. I know Mohammed is a Pathan tribesman, so I'm assuming it was their language called Pushto."

"Pathans? I thought Donohue was a rubber trader. Rubber is in Burma not in the Northwest Frontier, even I know that."

"There is a lot about Donohue we aren't going to know, pal.

Remember what the boss said about building a cover story. I suspect Donohue was all over India before the war and probably not as a rubber trader. All I know for sure is Mohammed is by no means a servant. He is Donohue's work partner, his bodyguard and a damn fine cook. He runs the local staff, keeps them out of our business and keeps track of the local neighborhood. I suspect he could cut our throats before we even knew he was angry. Anyhow, the boss is gone, and we will know more when he gets back. We can either stare at this mess, clean it up, or we can play some chess. What do you want to do first?"

Standish had proven to be a very good chess player, winning every time they played over the last two weeks. "I think cleaning up the mess is the right answer," O'Connell said.

Donohue and Mohammed returned two hours later. They were soaked in sweat after a late afternoon walk. They disappeared into different parts of the house to wash and change clothes. Donohue appeared just before sundown and met Standish and O'Connell on the veranda. He was dressed in a midnight blue silk shirt and European style cream colored linen trousers. Instead of his standard fabric Persian slippers, he wore woven leather sandals. "We will have some guests after dinner tonight. No cocktails tonight. We need to be sharp when they arrive. Please go change into whatever you have that resembles clothes used for respectable company."

O'Connell rolled his eyes and said, "I thought we were your respectable company, Boss."

"No Peter. You are my Honourable Company. Tonight we are entertaining and I don't want our guests to know immediately that you and Michael are the killers you really are."

Standish looked at Donohue. "Boss, any chance you are going to tell us what's going on?"

"No, Michael. This is my little surprise for you two."

In the previous two weeks, both O'Connell and Standish had visited Bombay tailors and they arrived at dinner in clothing similar to their boss' style. O'Connell was in a thin cotton shirt and black trousers and Standish wore khaki linen trousers and a light blue silk shirt with French cuffs. They stood at attention for "inspection" by their commander and after some adjustments, he agreed that their livery was "satisfactory." They had a quiet dinner of curry stuffed pakoras, cold meats and cheese with a pitcher of mango lassi to drink, and then moved to the library. As they entered the room, Donohue said something to Mohammed and closed the heavy teak double doors.

While this wasn't the first time O'Connell had been in the room referred to as "the library," it was the first time they had used the room in the center of the house for any of their discussions. French doors on the east wall opened on the veranda and the small, formal garden backed by the eight-foot-high wall. Large Central Asian carpets hung like tapestries on two walls. Tall bookcases were filled with leather bound books. Wooden ladders allowed access to the top shelves. Normally, the room had four wicker chairs known as planter's chairs because they were a cross between a chair and a chaise lounge. The chairs were designed with extra-long arm rests so a planter, or in the current situation, an OSS officer could put his feet up and doze while pretending to read the local newspapers. Instead, tonight the room had six wicker straight chairs surrounding a glass topped coffee table. There was a silver tray on the table with six fine china small coffee cups and saucers and a silver sugar bowl. Donohue looked at his square, gold wrist watch and said, "Our guests will arrive shortly. I want you to let me open the conversation without any drama. Understood?" O'Connell and Standish nodded.

Mohammed entered less than two minutes later with a silver and glass coffee pot in a small frame with a small can of Sterno underneath to keep it warm. The aroma of Turkish coffee filled the room. "Sir, the guests have arrived."

"Thank you, Mohammed. Please stand watch for us." Mohammed nodded and left the room.

The guests entered as he left. Two men and a woman. Their dark wool *shalwar kamiz* and wool scarves known as a *patou* did fit the local garb. It certainly did not disguise the fact that they were Europeans. The tallest and eldest of the three walked over to Donohue and shook his hand.

"Real John Buchan stuff, Patrick. Do you really think it was necessary, mate?" The speaker's Australian accent was tempered by years abroad. O'Connell thought: Canada? India? Some British Caribbean colony?

Donohue smiled and said, "John, we are working on a project that none of our British keepers would like. I just wanted to be sure that if you didn't want to play the game, you wouldn't be penalized."

"SOE Force 136 always wants to play, Patrick."

"Though I wonder if it is safe to work with this pirate. The last time I did, we almost ended up in Broadmoor Prison." O'Connell was surprised to hear the British accent of Clive Barker from under the patou of one of the other visitors.

"Clive! Once you healed, you were supposed to be fighting the Japs somewhere in Malaya. What in the world are you doing here?" Protocol might have argued for O'Connell to wait for introductions, but he was pleased to see a comrade in arms. He walked over, shook Barker's hand and put his left hand on Barker's shoulder. Barker leaned slightly into that pressure on the old wound, but did not wince. He was clearly back in action.

Donohue returned to the role of host and said, "John, the vocal one is my recent addition here, Major Peter O'Connell. I think you already know Major Michael Standish."

"Good to meet you, Peter. My name is Commander John Drake and I am head of Force 136 operations in Western India, based in Bombay. Greetings, Michael. I brought with me my new addition, Clive Barker, a recently promoted Major. Sapper by training and I have found to be an inveterate gambler by avocation. As you have guessed by now, he is another exile from the ETO. The third member of my party is Ensign Judith Kelly, nominally in the Field Ambulance Nursing Yeomanry assigned to my Royal Navy office in Bombay, but actually our only Force 136 agent in Goa under the alias Judith Connelly of the Eire Trading Company." Both Michael and Peter looked over at the third member of the SOE team who had pulled down her scarf to reveal copper hair and stunning green eyes.

"Gentlemen, focus on work if you please," Donohue said quietly as he walked toward the table and offer the SOE guests coffee.

Barker walked by O'Connell and whispered, "Jesus, Mary and Joseph, Peter! Have you never seen a girl before?" All O'Connell could do was blush.

After delivering coffee to the visitors and refilling his own cup, Donohue motioned to a library table covered with documents: Maps of the Indian coast and the Portuguese colony; city maps of Panjim and Vasco de Gama; agent reporting on MERCURY CORPO-RACOA; and a slightly redacted version of the DILETTANTE file. Once again, Mohammed had worked his magic arranging that portion of the room. O'Connell was reminded of Donohue's comments on how servants were often invisible to Europeans and Standish's guess that Mohammed could kill them before they even knew he was angry. All he knew for sure was it must be some sort of Asian magic.

Donohue started the conversation after he lighted a cigarette in his ivory holder. He motioned to others to smoke. Drake lit a pipe and Standish and Barker lit cigars. Kelly put a cigarette in her own ivory holder. O'Connell lit her cigarette with his Zippo lighter and then lit one for himself.

"John, I talked to you this afternoon in general about our little project. All the details we have are here. I wanted to start by stating that I see OPERATION DILETTANTE as good venue for mutual cooperation regardless of what OSS or SOE headquarters might think. I would like to offer a partnership with the understanding that I will not be reporting this partnership to our headquarters. I fear if you report it to your headquarters, you will not get approval to work with us and will likely get me into some hot water with OSS in New Delhi, Kandy and London. I wanted to be sure at the beginning that we are in agreement that everything we will tell our respective headquarters will be true, but highly edited. Agreed?"

"Patrick, I understand why you are being so formal, but I want you to know that I am in perfect agreement. Our little bit of fun will stay off the books and only the three of us in Force 136 will know about the project. It will mean delaying Barker's travel to the Malayan jungles, but I suspect he won't mind a bit of civilized work before he heads into headhunter country."

"No one told me there were headhunters!"

Drake smiled and said, "And they won't, old son. Only their Japanese victims know for sure."

Donohue returned to the purpose of the meeting by saying, "We will start with O'Connell describing our current understanding of our target, his company and the mission. You can read all of the details after his discussion. Our difficulty is getting into Goa and getting access to our target. John, I believe Ensign Kelly will be able to speak to those requirements."

"Sir, I will indeed." Judith Kelly's voice had a light Irish lilt as well as a clear note of confidence as she spoke up.

Standish shot an elbow into O'Connell's ribs and whispered, "Get to work, Peter, and if I were you, I would stop staring at Ensign Kelly."

O'Connell walked to the opposite side of the table so that he was facing the group and started to outline what they knew, what they thought, and what they didn't know about the mission, the target, and the operating environment. It took about an hour and another pot of the Turkish coffee. By the time he finished, the room was filled with smoke from Donohue's cigarette and Drake's pipe. Standish and Clive's cigars had long since gone out in ashtrays nearby.

O'Connell had worked hard to avoid focusing his conversation and his eyes on the female SOE ensign, but it hadn't been easy. This was not the first time that he had met a female agent. OSS and SOE operations in France had many female agents including some who were running their own local circuits. Other circuits included female wireless operators, chosen for their excellent French language and Morse code radio skills. The female radio operators could move their equipment from town to town with less chance of German or French collaborator scrutiny. O'Connell was aware a number of these women had been captured, tortured and shot in Northern and Central France though he hadn't known any of the victims. Now, he would be trusting his life and his operation to a woman who had been working undercover for months, perhaps years.

Drake spoke to the group. "I think we can help on a number of fronts. As you know, Patrick, we have had our share of operational successes in Goa especially OPERATION CREEK. We knocked out the Nazi submarine radio network all while avoiding any accusation that Britain violated Portuguese sovereignty. Well played, eh?"

Donohue responded, "I have been an admirer of CREEK for some time. You infiltrated Mormugao harbor, you destroyed the target ship, and bluffed the German and Italian crews of other Axis ships in the harbor to scuttle their vessels. Brilliant."

"Patrick, you don't know how clever the operation was because the real program remains secret. One thing I can say is that we have kept our infrastructure in place in Goa and Ensign Kelly manages that infrastructure from her office at Panjim Harbor. She is under cover as an Irish shipping agent, another neutral party, and has a network that certainly can augment your own agent network."

Donohue raised his hands, "John, what would make you think I am running an agent network out of Bombay. We both know that the British Raj would not approve."

"Right you are, Patrick. I'm sorry I even suggested it." Drake's Australian accent came through in his sarcasm. He turned to Kelly and said, "Judith, please let the gentlemen know the latest status of your operations in Goa."

"Our operation looks in many ways similar to Steinmark's operation. Judith Connelly, which is my alias in Goa, is the daughter of an Irish national running an import-export firm. It gives me an excuse to manage a small warehouse at Panjim Harbor as well as a bungalow in the city proper. While my work was substantially more complicated during CREEK, I have remained busy running an agent network focused on possible threats to Western India. Last year, MI6 shared a report with SOE headquarters that pointed to Traumann as a possible Nazi agent. We know that Major Steinmark is living under the alias of Traumann. It turns out that his warehouse is on the same street as our own. It is honestly just a coincidence that we are so close to the Nazi's warehouse. We were there first and the location was perfect for CREEK. It is also a good location for my radio communications out to sea."

"I have met him a few times during gatherings of both the business and international communities. He is charming and very successful in working the Portuguese authorities. Traumann is a known commodity there and his warehouse is always very busy, especially when ships come in from Portugal or Spain. When the occasional Brazilian cargo vessel arrives, there is more security at the warehouse courtesy of a number of local toughs. We suspect he pays healthy bribes to the local authorities, as do we, but his bribes and charisma must be brilliant because the authorities don't even pretend to inspect. About once a month, I get warned in advance that the inspectors are on their way and we clean up our warehouse and make sure there is an open crate of Irish whiskey near the front door. I have never seen any evidence they go near Steinmark's place." She paused to drink some of the Turkish coffee.

"As Patrick said earlier today when we first met, if I didn't know he was an Abwehr agent, I would have only assumed he was a successful Brazilian smuggler. Involved in crime to be sure, but no sign that he is a Nazi spy. I have been exploring whether he would be susceptible to switching sides. So far, all I can say for sure is that he has been more distracted the last few times I met him. I wonder if the changes in Berlin and the arrest of Canaris made him wonder about his own future. I think we can exploit this, but I'm not sure he will ever be recruited."

Drake nodded to Kelly and then continued, "Patrick, I think it is clear that we have the right capabilities in Goa to support the mission. The next step is yours. When do want to dispatch your men?"

"Gents, I don't want to be rude, but where do I enter into the picture?" This was the first time in an hour that Barker had spoken, and all eyes turned to him.

Drake answered, "Clive, Patrick and I were considering asking you to partner with O'Connell again. I understand you have some positive experience in him in France."

"And, what about me?" Now Standish was the speaker and everyone looked at him.

Donohue answered, "Michael, once I heard that John had Mr. Barker in play, I decided that DILETTANTE was not in your game book. Before you decide to complain, I also have some good news. John is managing a joint SOE-OSS enterprise called OPERATION CHARACTER. It is more or less like the Jedburgh teams except with the Karen tribesmen in Northern Burma."

Barker turned to Standish, "Remember the discussion of the head hunters?"

Donohue offered, "Michael, I seem to recall you did ask me to send you to Burma. I hope you find this satisfactory. You will be leaving the day after tomorrow on an Army Air Corps Dakota headed to Calcutta. After that, you will be travelling via an SOE aircraft. And, once DILETTANTE is successful, you should see both Mr. Barker and Peter in the area before too long."

Michael stood up and did theatrical bow, "I can see that all of my dreams have come true, thank you. Well, except for the head hunters…"

Drake spoke, "We made the headhunter story up, Michael. The headhunters are in another part of the 136 area of responsibility. At least, that is what I think I was told."

Donohue ended the joking by focusing the room back to the present. "Let's get back to work sorting out how to get Majors Barker and O'Connell into Goa and on target. It seems to me that we now have two choices. Both are good ones. Ensign Kelly can continue to pursue the recruitment option with Steinmark while our two commandos consider other options if he chooses not to say yes. Does that make sense?"

Drake nodded and they started to assemble a plan.

S teinmark walked through the warehouse as the newly arrived cargo containers were stacked by his men. Over the last year, he had worked hard to build his reputation as a legitimate shipping agent and the warehouse usually was filled with Brazilian products coming in or Goan products on their way out. This time, the warehouse was filled with industrial sized cargo containers that were only going to be stored temporarily before being transshipped. His men were no more or less interested in the new containers than previous shipments. From Steinmark's perspective, that was no bad thing.

By 1800hrs, the warehouse was quiet, the containers were in place and Steinmark was waiting in his office for his visitor. While he waited, he prepared his standard Portuguese Colonial Administration paperwork to pass the time. The left hand desk drawer was open with his Army issued Luger 9mm within easy reach.

"Dom Traumann?" The voice was slightly above a whisper though the silhouette in the shadows argued for a deeper and louder voice.

Steinmark answered in his best Brazilian accented Portuguese, "*Sim.*"

The shadow switched to German, "May I come in?"

"Please do." The shadow entered quietly and as he did, Steinmark slowly spun his desk lamp around so that now he was in the shadows and his visitor was on the edge of the illumination from the lamp.

The man was well over 180cm and looked to be nearly 100 kilos in weight, mostly in his shoulders and chest. Dressed in a dark wool suit and a black fedora hat, the man looked like the caricatures in the Nazi media of an enemy spy. He was definitely over dressed for a warm, late night in Goa. His face was covered in sweat. Despite his size and weight, he moved like a dancer and Steinmark noticed that the man approached with caution. Steinmark said, "Have a seat, my friend." The visitor took the one seat in the office outside the edge of the light from the desk lamp. Steinmark used his right hand to move the lamp. This was a game that could become tiresome.

The visitor continued in German and said, "Herr Steinmark, I want to talk to you about the cargo shipment you received today. I believe it is destined for delivery to my ship."

Steinmark replied in German, "Sir, my name is Traumann and I need to see some sort of documentation before we can go any farther. I run, after all, a legitimate import and export firm and need a bill of lading that argues that the shipment is yours."

"Herr Steinmark, we both know you are far more than an importer in this colony, but I realize you want to confirm who I am. With your permission, I will reach into my coat to get my credentials."

Steinmark thought, this is one careful player. He moved his chair so that his left hand was hidden from view and rested on the grip of the Luger in the drawer. He waved agreement with his right hand. He said, "Of course. However, I do want you to know that I think this mission is not in order. Our nations are enemies. Still, I have my orders. Since the dispatch did not give your name, how shall I call you?"

The visitor smiled revealing a pair of gold front teeth as he handed over a copy of paperwork that appeared to have its origins in Berlin. He said, "Just call me Comrade Vanya."

O'Connell and Barker's travel to Goa was uneventful and uncomfortable. Donohue's network of travelers arranged delivery down the Malabar Coast using a lorry that was a veteran of the First World War. Barker recognized the painted over markings almost immediately as they rode in the back of the truck behind a ton of mangoes, vegetables and eggs.

"Brother O'Connell, I noticed this truck served the Indian Army in the Great War. It probably drove up the Euphrates River in 1916. It is a wonder that it is still running."

"Given the speed we are making along this dirt road, I am not sure it is running at all. I suspect it is being pulled by water buffalo."

"No chance, mate. I know what the fumes from a poorly running gasoline engine smells like. I promise you this is it."

"Which is why I am slightly green and enjoying this trip far less than any previous travels with the OSS."

They eventually made it to a fishing village one hundred miles south of Bombay and waited a day in a small hut owned by another of Donohue's network. On 20 November, a coal powered coastal trawler that could only be described as another remnant of the Great War pulled into the dock at the village and took on the two special operations officers and their duffle bags filled with supplies. They had now transitioned into the Force 136 network and spent a day and a night in the hold of the boat as it moved down the coast to Goa. The

Portuguese authorities were familiar with the boat and the skipper and for a small exchange of several crates of mangoes from India, they were authorized entry into Panjim harbor. On 21 November, smelling of fish and coal smoke, O'Connell and Barker arrived at the Force 136 warehouse within sight of the warehouse of MERCURY CORPORACOA. After a cold-water bath in a rubber tub and a change of clothes, they went to sleep on the top floor of their new home.

Judith Kelly arrived the next day with food, additional clothing, and a report on the actions of their target. She was dressed in a cotton frock that made her look even younger than her 25 years. Her red hair was pulled into a bun and she wore white canvas boat shoes known in the British Empire as plimsolls. Her entire appearance made Peter O'Connell tremble. She was beautiful.

Over tea in their new home, Kelly provided the details, "Gents, welcome to Eire Shipping and Handling: Yours truly, Judith Connelly, welcomes you to a bit of the Irish Republic. I manage the company and do a brisk business trading Irish product for Goan fruits and vegetables. I suspect by the end of the war, we will have made a tidy profit on the exchange. We definitely don't need His Majesty's Government to fund us for at least the next year," Kelly winked as she offered the two men a second cup of coffee and two very large Portuguese pastries.

She pointed out the window and about 200 yards away was the MERCURY CORPORACOA warehouse. "The warehouse serves as both the storage venue and Steinmark's office. As I said in Bombay, he is well respected here. I met him again last Sunday at a reception at the Harbor Master's bungalow. He is charming and discrete. He works hard to maintain his story of the middle aged, German expatriate Brazilian trader. He has shown some interest in me, well… in Judith Connelly. I hope to build a better picture of Steinmark as a person over the next week. There may be an opening to recruit Steinmark. That said, I have no idea what is inside the warehouse."

"So, our first job is a bit of work to find out what's inside?" Barker said as he poured his third cup of coffee and added enough milk to make the coffee the color of caramel.

"Exactly what I was going to suggest. You commandos know how to do the needful without using any demolitions?" Judith smiled.

"Clive always prefers to use demo, but I think in this case, we can use quieter techniques to get inside," O'Connell said. "What do you expect us to find?"

"I don't know for sure. It could be Aladdin's cave with anything from sophisticated radio equipment, to crates of German guns for the Japs in Burma to sacks of gold and jewels. I don't even know for sure if there are guards inside. I absolutely know there are guards outside day and night." She pointed out the window to the street where O'Connell and Barker could see a half dozen large men.

"Pirates?" Barker used his best radio drama Long John Silver imitation to express his thoughts.

O'Connell added, "None have a peg leg, but I do notice they are all carrying cutlasses."

Kelly said, "It's called a *klewang*. Carried by Indonesian pirates and other ne'er do wells of the Malaccan coast. They are weighted at the front for chopping and sharp as a razor. My father was in the Singapore Police before the war. He always said, shoot the guy with the klewang first. I think Steinmark brought in his own team to guard the place rather than use Goans or South Indians. I recognized some of them as Indonesians, some as Malaysians and some look to be from East Africa. I've tried to engage them in a couple of different languages. They haven't succumbed to my charms yet."

"Well, maybe we will watch the warehouse for a day or so before we decide which of these pirates we shoot first, eh?" Barker reached into his duffle and pulled out a pair of Royal Navy binoculars. "If we set up a table near this window and keep our wits about us, we should be able to use this as an observation post for the next 48 hours. Assuming we have good luck, that should tell us enough to know how to get into the warehouse."

"And how much plastic explosive we need to use." O'Connell couldn't help but add to the discussion.

Barker ignored his partner and turned to their host, "Judith, is there any chance of acquiring a crossbow in the next couple of days?"

"Crossbow? I don't know if there are any in Goa. They are common enough among the tribals in Burma and French Indo-China, but I don't know about Goa. I will get the word out."

Barker said, "And, could you bring tea next time? I know coffee is more common here, but take pity on your fellow Brit."

"Weakling," was all O'Connell had to say about his choice of beverage.

F or three days and nights, O'Connell and Barker shared the room overlooking the warehouse, with Kelly visiting regularly to supply food and information. They kept a log of comings and goings at the warehouse and the level of diligence shown by the guards. They had a chance to see Steinmark when he arrived on 23 November in his black Mercedes limousine driven by another of his entourage of pirates. He was dressed in an immaculate cream-colored linen suit with a matching straw fedora, dark sunglasses and a walking stick. He arrived at noon and stayed until just before dark. Since the warehouse had no windows, they could only guess which part of the building he visited.

Their hostess returned the morning of 25 November with a flask of hot coffee, another of hot tea, and Portuguese pastries. Conversation was delayed as O'Connell and Barker emptied their mugs and devoured the pastries. Kelly said, "You act like you haven't been fed in days. I just brought you dinner last night for goodness sake."

O'Connell waited a moment as he finished his pastry and jam. "It's hard work sitting up all night watching and keeping logs of the guards, their shift changes and the comings and goings on the street," he said.

"And he has to keep me amused for the entire night," Barker added. "I'm not sure the Yank sleeps. Story upon story of his life in the States and his adventures in Italy. You would think I was a perfect stranger. He even told me stories from France where I am the main character."

"Now I am hurt, Clive. Here I was trying to educate you on life in America and all I get is complaints."

Kelly laughed, "You two sound like an old married couple instead of a pair of commandos. I hope there is actually some work that comes out of this."

Barker finished his coffee and said, "Judith, we know enough about the warehouse to know that we are going to have to approach it from the sea not the street. Those pirates never stop their patrols, in pairs, shifting personnel every 4 hours. They just don't stop. Looking at the port map you gave us, I think our best route into the warehouse is at the dock."

Barker ignored the interruption and continued, "The guards appear to be only covering the front entrance rather than conducting a patrol around the warehouse. I suspect they have a sea-side team as well, but the map shows that the quay has a number of docking positions and we should be able to get a small boat near enough to one of the moorings so we can make a quick hop to the warehouse sea side door. Like little thieves of the Arabian nights we will carefully enter Aladdin's cave and see what we can see. Of course, we may have to eliminate one of the guards, but accidents happen on the docks and people do fall into the water. Dangerous business shipping. Which, by the way, is why I want a crossbow."

Barker finished the last pastry and said, "I'm off to bed. I will let you two figure out how and when we can get a small boat up to the dock. Judith, consider yourself warned that he is going to tell you his life story growing up in a city called Buffalo." He wandered off to the office space that had their two bunks.

"It won't be as bad as that, I promise." O'Connell said in his most polite voice.

Once Barker left, O'Connell started asking Kelly more detailed questions on Steinmark.

"Every time I see him, I realize how lonely he must be," she said.

"He has superficial relationships with all of the Portuguese officials here, but he doesn't seem to have any close friends. I wonder if I should approach him directly to arrange a meeting where you, Clive and I could have a chat. He certainly appears to have mixed feelings about his life here."

"I suspect some of your observations are based on the fact that he finds your company more pleasant than his official contacts." O'Connell had tried to make the remark appear off-hand, but it didn't work. It sounded like something that might come out of the mouth of a jealous teenager.

"Don't be daft, Peter. I am working this target for a reason. Steinmark is a Nazi intelligence officer. We don't know for sure why he came here last year, but his mission had to be designed to harm the Empire. Drake and Donohue made it clear that we should try to recruit Steinmark. If that doesn't work, then we will eliminate him. Right now, that's my reason for being here."

O'Connell stared at this feet. "Apologies. I just figured...."

Kelly's green eyes flashed with anger.

"I know what you figured, Peter. Let me explain. I may look young, but that is a function of family traits not calendar years. Some of you commandos seem to see me just as a person to serve tea, but, let me be clear. I have been working for the SOE since 1940. I started as a radio operator in central France in 1941. My circuit was wrapped up by the Germans. I was the only survivor and that was because I knifed the two GESTAPO men who arrived in the middle of one of my transmissions. London decided they needed a good operator in Goa to support CREEK. My family is from Armagh on the border with the Irish Republic. I speak Gaelic, my mum and dad were killed in the blitz while I was in France, so I don't have a lot to keep me in England."

"So, Eire Shipping and Handling was born, and the "fragile" Dublin maid named Judith Connelly is running it for her father. CREEK taught me how a careful plan can win against long odds.

Now, if the goal is to eliminate Steinmark from the chessboard, then I intend to be part of the equation. Whatever it takes."

O'Connell was taken aback by the strength of her chastisement and realized he had been wrong about Judith Kelly. It wasn't clear if he could dig himself out of the hole he was in anytime soon. "I'm sorry," he said. "I didn't mean anything."

"Peter, one of the reasons that I have been as effective as an SOE agent and one of the reasons I am alive today is because I don't look like some Mata Hari or like some commando. It turns out that I have skills I never realized before the war while I was in university. You probably haven't seen a women do this sort of job."

O'Connell thought about the French resistance leader Jocelyn Montreux: Under twenty, leading a resistance unit and, most probably part of the plot to kill him to fulfill the communist mission. He had to admit, he had misunderstood Montreux and, now he had misunderstood Kelly. He said, "I have seen some women in the field. I guess I am just not used to it."

"Were you brought up in some basement in that town of Buffalo?"

O'Connell flushed and blurted out, "I went to a boys Catholic School and then to Canisius College which is a Catholic College. Except for my mother and nuns, I don't have a lot of experience with women."

"More or less naïve in your own way. Eh, Peter?" Kelly started to laugh.

"Now you are pulling my leg, and it is clear you aren't quite as mad as you seemed. One final question, why not use your real name Judith Kelly?"

"Peter, there really is a Patrick Connelly who really worked on the docks in the Irish Republic and had a daughter named Judith, but she died as a child in the 1920s flu epidemic. Once the war started, Connelly was approached by the Germans to revive an IRA network in Belfast and Liverpool. He made a mistake and accepted the mission and he ended up in the hands of Special Branch. The Connelly story matched what we needed for CREEK and I was the only SOE Irish lass available at the time. So, for now and for you, *I am* Judith Connelly."

She paused, her eyes softening, "Now, again to be clear, I am interested in your life story and once we get finished here, I will take you to a beach where we can share those tales. Now, you need to focus and I have to find a way for you to go out to sea and then bring a boat into the harbor. Do you know what a folboat is?"

"Trained with one at the OSS school. Basically a two man canvas kayak, right?"

"Exactly. We have two in the warehouse which are leftovers from another Force 136 mission. Still in their crates, so we have to do an inspection, but I think that should solve your problems. When do you intend to make your visit?"

"When can you arrange for our transportation?"

"Tonight too soon? I have a connection with the fishing fleet that leaves tonight. They will cruise out of the harbor and stop at the entrance buoy to let you off. Sound okay?"

"Swell. Let's check the folboat and then I'm going to hit the rack and try to get some sleep. You do know that Clive snores, right?"

"As I said, like an old married couple," Kelly said as she led O'Connell down the stairs to the warehouse proper where the folboats were stored along with some tools of the trade for the two commandos.

"By the way, I have a date with Steinmark tonight. While you are exploring his Aladdin's Cave, I will be exploring his personal secrets."

Judith Kelly, living as Judith Connelly, spent the evening at a hillside restaurant with her target, Jan Steinmark living as Maximilian Traumann. Over their second bottle of Portuguese white wine, she asked him, "Do you intend to stay here after the war? Personally, I think our days of making profits in this neutral colony will end as soon as the Brits win. They will open the borders and I don't think my firm is going to survive if goods can come from England by way of India.

It's really only a matter of time and my own view is that it is time to make some decisions about the future."

Steinmark played with his wine glass. After nearly a minute of silence, he said, "I don't know what happens next for my company."

Since their best shared language was French, Kelly wasn't sure if that short response was due to Steinmark's indecision or because of his language skill. She gently pressed on, "We could join forces and create a company that would link Ireland with Brazil."

Steinmark looked her in the eyes. Kelly noticed that when Steinmark got tired he was less successful keeping his glass eye in line with his left eye. "That might be possible, but I have at least one or two more shipments coming from Brazil in the next few weeks. They should create enough profit for me to consider leaving Goa. Can you wait?"

Kelly's training in agent operations had been limited in 1940 to building simple networks for escape and evasion routes. This was the first time she had worked against a rival intelligence officer. She knew one thing for certain: Delaying the inevitable confrontation would not help. "I don't think my company would wait for weeks. Days, perhaps. But weeks, I don't think so. My father's Dublin connections are focused on a post-war world and they want to sort out my role in it soon. Maximillian, I think you should consider my offer sooner rather than later."

Steinmark looked at the watch on his wrist. It was midnight. "Dear Judith. I will answer your question tomorrow. Perhaps a late lunch at Phillip's café? He uses fresh fish from the fishing fleet. Would that be satisfactory?"

"Maximillian, that would be lovely. Would you like to join me for games of chance at the casino?"

"I know it may seem strange, but I have to return to work. Tomorrow morning I have a ship arriving from Brazil just after Mass. If we are going to have lunch tomorrow, I would prefer to complete the necessary papers for the Portuguese authorities tonight."

Kelly suspected there was a reason for Steinmark to return to his warehouse, but probably not for paperwork. She knew O'Connell and Barker were already on their way to the same location if not already in the warehouse. She smiled and said, "Not even an hour at the casino?"

"Perhaps an hour, but no longer." He stood up, walked over to Connelly and moved her chair and then wrapped her in her silk and wool Kashmiri shawl. "Just an hour, my dear, then I must return to work."

As they walked toward the casino, Steinmark silently mulled over his current situation. In the most recent radio transmission, Berlin had identified his dinner partner as a British agent. Her cover story of "Judith Connelly, daughter of Patrick Connelly" was completely false. Connelly's daughter had died years before and he was currently in British custody. Given that she was a British agent, her offer of a joint operation could only mean that the Aliies were aware that he was a German agent. It was a game of cat-and-mouse, and, for now, he believed he was the cat. Connelly, or whatever her true name, was a charming young woman and had played her hand gently. It was a game worth playing, though he knew he would have to refuse her offer soon. For the sake of his mission, he would have to identify some way to disrupt her residency here in Goa. Perhaps the placement of a dead body in her warehouse? Even if the evidence didn't point to her, it would force the Portuguese authorities to investigate — especially after he supplied them with the right information.

Steinmark did not want to harm the woman, but he intended to drive her out of Goa before she could harm him. He doubted she knew of his link to the Soviet officer, but it was clear she was offering him an opportunity to escape his current dilemma and would continue to press him to change sides. He might not be a Nazi, but he was not a traitor. Miss Connelly could not be allowed to investigate his actions as he continued the mission to set up the exfiltration route for the German leadership. If all else failed, he would take care of the young woman himself. He would do everything in his power to avoid that choice, but he knew he would make it if necessary.

As to her offer of escape, Steinmark already had his own smuggling network in place, a sailboat and his new passport. At any point in the future, he could escape without help from the British.

Kelly noticed Steinmark's silence as they walked to the casino. She said, "Max, you seem a million miles away."

"I was just considering your offer. It is very interesting and we need to talk about this more tomorrow at lunch. Can we meet at 2 at the café?

"Max, that sounds like a wonderful plan."

26 November 1944. Harbor buoy, Panjim

As Kelly's fishing trawler passed the harbor entrance buoy, the captain stopped just long enough to launch the folboat. Barker looked at the radium dial on his watch. It was half past midnight. He figured they had a half hour to get to the docks, no more than 90 minutes inside the warehouse and then 30 minutes back to a rendezvous site in the mangrove swamps north of the harbor. Even with delays, they would be at the rendezvous at 0400hrs.

The folboat was large enough for the two men and a small bag of equipment. The boat looked and acted just like a kayak used by native hunters in the Arctic Ocean. The paddlers sat knelt inside the craft, balancing on thin wicker seats, with a waterproof canvas sleeve pulled tight against them kept water from flooding the small boat. O'Connell, in the front position, supplied most of the power with the double-bladed paddle. Barker was in the back using his paddle to steer and keep on course by watching the large, radium dialed compass attached to the hull between the two seats. He claimed that his recent shoulder wound made him less capable as a paddler. O'Connell wasn't convinced.

"This is the first time I've done this in open water." O'Connell said between strokes.

"Perfect. What did you do in OSS school, paddle about in a swimming pool?"

"No, wise guy. We used the Potomac River and the Navy yards in

Norfolk but we always launched from shore and stayed well within sight of the beach."

"Peter, if you stick with me after this job, Force 136 spends plenty of time in folboats. I have been informed that this is how we travel to shore from submarine or motor torpedo boats, MTBs in our parlance and PT boats in yours. It is the only way to get into the fight other than trying to parachute into triple-canopy jungle." Barker looked down at the compass and said, "And pull more with your left arm, we are going off course."

"Always the critic, eh?"

O'Connell and Barker approached the docks after 45 minutes of hard paddling. Barker whispered as they got near the mooring for Steinmark's building, "Next time, I suppose I should check the tide tables."

O'Connell looked back, "You mean I have been working against the tide as well as carrying you?"

"A slight error in reading the tables. Hey, I'm not Royal Navy, remember?"

They pulled under the dock and roped the folboat to a ladder leading up to the mooring midway across the boat. O'Connell held the boat steady and Barker climbed the first six rungs of the ladder and then steadied the boat while Peter climbed on the ladder. Face to face on opposite sides of the ladder, they took a few breathes before climbing up to the dock.

"After you," Barker said in his best imitation of an aristocratic accent.

"It only seems fair to let you go first since you were the one who steered us to this spot. You should find out first if this is even close to the right location."

"Mustn't moan, mate." Barker said over his shoulder as he climbed up the ladder until his head cleared the concrete dock. "No sign of any guards at this end and, just in case you were wondering, we are directly in front of the warehouse."

"Amazing, Clive. Now what?"

"Follow me," Barker said as he cleared the concrete mooring, staying on his stomach to keep the lowest possible profile. O'Connell followed him until they were both on the edge of the dock. He pulled a climbing rope up from the folboat, carrying their gear including Barker's newly acquired crossbow. Barker assembled the bow and rested an eight inch bolt into place. Peter pulled out his High Standard pistol. They got up and ran quickly to the warehouse man door next to the large cargo door that would be used to load and unload equipment.

"Now it's your turn to demonstrate some skills," Barker whispered in O'Connell's ear as they leaned against the wall of the warehouse. O'Connell knelt on one knee and pulled out the set of lock picks issued at the OSS training facility. As he worked, the onshore winds started to pick up. Barker looked at the sky and said, "It would be nice if we could get in here before it started to rain."

O'Connell looked up and said, "It doesn't rain here in the fall." He was in the door in under 30 seconds.

"Slick, my boy." The first of many very large rain drops hit Barker in the head.

O'Connell looked over his shoulder and said, "It was easy."

They opened the door carefully to see if there was any light inside. Just as they did, the sky opened, and a downpour started. Ready or not, they decided it was time to get in out of the rain. There were no office lights or signs of life in the warehouse, they closed the door behind them and entered the pitch-dark space. They each had a waterproof flashlight courtesy of the SOE supplies from Panjim. When they turned them on, they were surprised at the result.

"This really is bloody Aladdin's cave," Barker exclaimed. The light from their torches revealed three rows of shipping crates with an inventory list attached to the first crate in each row. Every one of the wooden crates had German Gothic style lettering and a Swastika painted on the side. O'Connell checked the inventory list for the first row. His rudimentary high-school German delivered the necessary knowledge: Weapons. On the list were a type of German rifle, named the *Sturmgewehr* 44, and German anti-tank weapons, the *Panzerschreck* and the *Panzerfaust*. The inventory showed the row to have 10 of each weapon in each crate and a crate of the appropriate ammunition.

The inventory in the second row listed aircraft engine parts for an aircraft named *Schwalbe*. The third row simply listed each box by weight and the material: Gold.

O'Connell looked at his watch and said, "We have time, we should open a box from each row to see what's really inside."

Barker walked up with two crowbars in his hands and said, "I'm taking the third row first."

O'Connell smirked, "Just remember you don't want a lot of weight in your pockets when we go back out to sea. And, because of your misreading of the tides, we don't have more than an hour to make this happen." He walked to the second crate in the first row, pried open the box, reached in, and pulled out one of the rifles. Magazine fed more like his Thompson than his Garand, light-weight, and with a pistol grip. "I'm going to see if I can find some ammo for this." He walked over to the last crate in the row and took out a box of the cartridges identified for the weapon, opened the box and loaded rounds into the magazine. "We might want this before the night is through," he said as he sealed up the box.

"Mother of God!" was all he heard from two rows over. O'Connell ran over to find Barker holding two canvas bags of coins marked Bank of England. He said, "Gold coins. Each of these bags has a stencil on the side in English that says the weight is ten pounds. This crate weighs 250 kilos, so each crate has over 500 pounds of gold." Barker held up a bag and looked at its markings. "Peter, that means each crate is worth a million British Pounds. What in bloody hell is this doing here?"

In the dim light from the two flashlights, he could see Barker's confused face and he didn't have an answer to the question. Instead, he said, "Look at this weapon, Clive. It is brand new and I'm not sure I've ever seen anything like it."

Clive took the weapon from Peter's hand, put down the flashlight so that it provided him enough light to do a function check and shoulder the weapon. "Brilliant," was all he said.

"OK, close up the bank and let's see what the middle row has to offer."

They worked down the middle row of much larger crates. They picked a crate at random and opened it.

"I've never seen an engine like this before and my German is crap. What the hell is a *Schwalbe*?"

Barker shook his head, "It means Swallow. But, what sort of engine has a rotor inside the housing but no drive shaft coming out of either end? And look at the tubing inside. It is obviously a fuel delivery system and a set of fans but where is the propeller?"

Barker dug deeper into the crate and found a large technical manual wrapped in waxed cloth. He opened it and started to read it. "It is some sort of rocket engine, Peter. Like Buck Rogers."

"Well, we can't take the engine, but we can take the manual. Let's close this up and get out of here before the owners arrive."

"Not before I leave a little something behind, Peter." Barker reached into his shoulder bag and pulled out a small limpet mine with a time pencil. He reached deep into the crate, so deep that his feet left the ground. O'Connell heard the distinctive snap of metal on metal as the magnet on the limpet mine connected. Barker's head appeared as his feet touched the ground.

"It wasn't easy. The entire engine is aluminum, but the frame holding it in the crate is steel. I used a twenty-four hour time pencil fuse. We will be history before that one goes off."

O'Connell nodded and said, "You want to place a couple more in the crates?"

"Demolitions are an art as well as a science. I am confident this one will blow up. But the answer to your question is: yes, because of the old adage two is one and one is none. Open another of the crates in this row."

They used the crowbar to open a crate at the end of the row. Once again, Barker reached deep inside and set the charge. "My two little presents represent slightly more than a kilo of plastic explosive each. At the very least, it will make a racket." They hammered the nails back into the top of the crates and started to work their way toward the dock-side door when they heard noise from the opposite end of the warehouse.

The door at the street side of the warehouse opened with a cry of steel on steel. Apparently the owners didn't believe in oiling hinges and the sound saved O'Connell and Barker from being discovered.

They ran into the far corner of the warehouse, reaching a wall of tool cabinets and lockers just as a pair of men carrying flashlights walked into the warehouse. They were speaking in German, with one struggling in what was clearly his second language. Barker tried to keep O'Connell up to speed on the discussion by whispering in his ear.

"If the first Joe isn't Steinmark, then he is Steinmark's boss. He talks like this is his place. The second Joe is not German and definitely not Portuguese. He seems to be driving a hard bargain with the first Joe." The conversation continued as the two men walked around the warehouse. Barker continued, "It sounds like they are arranging some sort of trade. The first Joe said he is working for the second Joe only because he is under orders to do so. The orders were an exchange: Some of his mates safe passage in exchange for the goods. The other Joe is saying, that only works after this delivery. After that, then he can arrange for their safe passage to…balls." Barker looked at O'Connell. "The second Joe is promising safe passage and a new life in Moscow."

"Commies. I hate Commies," O'Connell whispered. Then, "OK, so do we kill these two Joes now or do we wait?"

"You were the one who wondered why I brought a crossbow." Just as Barker finished reloading the bolt in the crossbow, they heard the main cargo door open. Light flooded the main warehouse space leaving their end in shadows. They heard the footsteps of at least twenty men along with two small chain fork lifts being pushed into the warehouse.

"Too late, it would appear," was all O'Connell could say as he and Barker pushed back deeper into the workshop area.

They sat in the warehouse for two hours worried every minute that they would be discovered. O'Connell couldn't take his eyes off his watch as the hands moved closer and closer to their designated rendezvous time with the fishing trawler. The twenty men, all dressed like pirates from a Douglas Fairbanks movie, began to move crates from the warehouse, through the cargo door on the dock-side and out to some sort of ship. They used wheeled dollies to move the crates from the row that housed the money and two out of the three crates from the middle row of aircraft engines. While Steinmark was supervising, Barker noted that the Russian speaker pulled one of African "pirates" aside for conversation. O'Connell saw it as well. It looked like a negotiation that did not include Steinmark. They were too far away to hear any of the conversation.

After the cargo was shifted, the "pirates" closed the cargo door, walked across the warehouse to the man door on the street side, shut off the lights, and closed up. Barker and O'Connell remained hidden for another fifteen minutes to be sure no one was going to return. O'Connell checked his watch for the twentieth time since they started hiding. It was 0445hrs. Even if they left immediately, they would miss their rendezvous. After another fifteen minutes of silence, they decided it was safe to move.

"So, what do we do next?" O'Connell said as he tried to loosen his muscles after hours of sitting still.

"First thing I'm going to do is pee before I wet myself," was all Barker said as he walked behind the remaining crates. Peter couldn't argue that point and walked to another corner of the building. As they walked, both men counted the crates as they passed. When they finally returned, they shared their count.

"I reckon they took half the gold and all of the aircraft parts. It doesn't appear that they took any of the weapons," Barker looked down at his notebook using his flashlight. "For sure, they took the crates with my small additions."

"Agreed. You have any more of your little toys that we can leave behind? I would hate to think all we leave behind now is pee."

"Not to worry, mate. I had a couple of incendiaries left in the bag.

I put them over next to a set of gasoline cans near my informal WC. The incendiaries will start the fire and the gasoline should do the job."

"So, now we have to get on the dock and look for the ship they loaded."

"Thank you, Major Obvious. I never would have thought of that."

"You are just grumpy you didn't get to use the crossbow."

"Yet."

They moved to the door on the dock-side and opened it an inch to peer out into the rainy night. It was nearly dawn, but there was nothing but dark sky and rain. No one was visible on the dock. As soon as the door opened, the smell of fish, diesel oil, and human waste entered the building.

"No sign of a guard on either side of the door. Willing to chance it, Yank?"

"Given the choice of another night shoulder to shoulder next to you among the bat guano, I think I will give it a chance."

"It was bird droppings and rat shit. I know the difference."

"Training?"

"Experience in a Catholic bell tower in France. Good place to send radio transmissions, bad place if you don't like bats." All O'Connell could do was shiver at the thought.

O'Connell pulled the German assault rifle off his shoulder and carefully chambered a round. He noticed there was a safety selector switch was on the left side of the pistol grip and the shoulder strap was designed to allow the owner to fire from the hip. He put the weapon on safe. As Barker opened the door, he passed through and found himself face to face with a very large, very wet, very angry guard leaning against the wall unsuccessfully avoiding the downpour.

When Barker worked his own way out, he saw O'Connell and one of Steinmark's guards in what could only be described as a "dance of death." The guard had at least three inches on O'Connell's frame and probably twenty pounds. They were fighting for control of each other's hands while trying hard to stab each other. Peter had pulled his Mark II fighting knife and the guard wielded a curved eight-inch blade. As they worked their dance away from the wall, Barker put a bolt in the crossbow. He shouted, "Break free!" As O'Connell moved away from the guard, Barker aimed carefully and shot. The bolt went through the guard's neck and he dropped like a marionette whose strings had been cut.

"You're welcome," Barker said as he walked to check the guard.

They wasted no time getting the body off the dock and into the water. Once that job was done, they were down the ladder and into the folboat. They were both pleased and surprised to see that it was still in place given the storm and the tidal shifts that could have bashed the sides of the fragile craft against the concrete dock. They paddled under the docks until they were a half mile from the warehouse, then headed to the rendezvous site in the mangrove swamp just on the edge of the port. They were now more than an hour off schedule, but Barker said their SOE counterpart would have offered the fisherman enough that he would wait all day if necessary. After all: No commandos, no money.

They reached the rendezvous location after a long paddle through the driving rain. The rain did not stop ship traffic, so they had to wait at one of the harbor buoys as a cargo ship headed out to sea. Once they crossed the shipping channel the waves and the rain made their little folboat nearly invisible. O'Connell paddled like his life depended on it and, perhaps, it did given the fact that the waves were washing over the boat and threatening to fill it with sea water. The rain finally stopped just as they pulled toward the coast. It was 0725hrs and the hot morning sun began to beat down on their backs as they paddled toward the swamp. The smell of the rotting vegetation in the thick mangroves was terrible, but they forgot the smell as soon as they saw a much larger trawler waiting at the RV.

O'Connell was the first to speak, "Personally, I'm happy to be finished with this paddling-like-mad job."

Barker said, "I suppose you didn't notice Judith at the railing. She is with the crew and that had to make you happy."

"Well, there was that."

As they pulled themselves over the cargo net and onto the fishing trawler, O'Connell and Barker realized that not only was Judith onboard, but Donohue, Mohammed and Drake were on deck waiting for them. All three were in foul-weather gear that belonged more on a Royal Navy destroyer than an Indian coastal trawler, but in the steady rain which started again almost on cue, no one would notice. What Barker did notice was the cold, steady glare he got from Drake. He whispered to O'Connell as they pulled the folboat on board and secured their little kayak to the deck, "Mate, this can't be good."

A new squall of heavy rain washed across the deck. Donohue and Drake waved for the two new arrivals to head into the small pilot house at the rear of the trawler. As with the previous trawler that dropped them off, this one smelled of diesel oil, shellac, rotting fish and curry. At least it was dry.

They followed Donohue past the captain's station and slid down the small set of stairs to an even smaller room below decks. Mohammed stayed with the local captain in the pilot house. Donohue motioned for O'Connell and Barker to sit at the chart table that served as captain's quarters, crew mess, and navigation center. A small oil lamp cast a yellow glow in the cabin as the daylight receded under the storm. Judith and Drake pulled up two more chairs around the table. It was a tight fit with shoulder's touching all around. O'Connell and Barker were soaked to the skin with their hair plastered to their heads mirroring the sodden black watch caps that they had taken off as soon as they entered the trawler. O'Connell noticed that Donohue had made sure that he was directly across from O'Connell and that Barker faced his SOE chief. Judith could always be a distraction regardless of where she was in the room. In this case, she was behind O'Connell, which made it easier to keep focused and answer any questions from Donohue.

Donohue started, "Gentlemen, we were more than a bit worried when you didn't make the rendezvous early this morning. Judith sent a radio message and John was kind enough to get us access to a Royal Navy MTB. We made landfall north of here an hour ago and Judith picked us up. It is no longer early morning, and I would like to ask every so politely, where in the world have you been? I have lost most of what little hair I have left on my head worrying about you. "

Drake added, "We realize that time schedules are just approximations of what you intend to follow, but over three hours late is more than we could expect."

O'Connell decided to start the explanation with little preamble and certainly no apologies. They were happy to be alive and that was that. "Gentlemen, we were delayed inside the Steinmark warehouse for over two hours waiting for the activity in the warehouse to conclude. Once it did conclude, we left and paddled here as fast as we could."

O'Connell paused for a breath. Drake used that moment to ask, "Barker, what exactly were you doing in the warehouse when you were...delayed."

"Sir, we were hiding in the warehouse so that we didn't get cut to shreds by Steinmark's pirates." In the background, Judith barely stifled a giggle. Donohue wanted to get the story from start to finish, so he said, "Major O'Connell, I believe you need to give us the full story, if you please, with no editorial comments."

O'Connell spent the next thirty minutes explaining what they did, what they saw and what they heard. He pulled out of an oilskin pocket the manual for the German aircraft engine. While Donohue and Drake were digesting the schematics, O'Connell asked permission to retrieve another item from their folboat. In the rain, he went back on deck and pulled the German assault rifle out of the boat. Before he left the deck, he noticed four bags of gold sovereigns in the rucksack under the wicker seats. He decided not to bring them in.

"Sir, when we left, all the crates of these rifles and half the crates of gold were still in the warehouse. We decided that they should be destroyed before the Germans could pass them on to the Russians."

Drake took his pipe out of his mouth and looked directly at Barker, "Destroyed? You decided to destroy these new rifles?"

"Sir, I assumed there would be no proper way for us to acquire all of the rifles for our use and didn't have any proof that they were going to any allied cause. So, I took responsibility and decided that the best course of action was to destroy them." He looked at his watch and said, "Of course, if you have the means to raid the warehouse to acquire the rifles, we still have almost six hours to do so before the fire starts."

Judith Kelly offered an opinion for the first time. "Steinmark might be willing to come over to our side if given a chance. He seems on the edge. We have a lunch date this afternoon. There is a chance we might acquire all of the warehouse goods after that."

Drake shook his head, "We know a portion of this shipment is already on its way to somewhere else. Judith, I think we must acquire these weapons before they get into the wrong hands. After that, you can continue to pursue Steinmark as a recruitment target." He turned to Barker again and said, "How many guards on the quay?"

"None when we left, sir. We had a little trouble on our departure and the quay side guard ended up in the water. He won't be getting back on the dock."

"So, there is nothing to stop us from taking those rifles now."

This time O'Connell commented, "Sir, we have no way of knowing what is waiting at the dock at this point. We do know that whatever ship was loaded early this morning is already anchored out somewhere in the harbor. We don't know if there will be another ship loading the rifles or if that is for another day."

Drake turned to Donohue, "Patrick, I think we can,…no," Drake paused, "we *must* try to get as many of those rifles as we can." Drake tapped the tobacco out of his pipe to emphasize his point.

Donohue looked at Drake and then at O'Connell and Barker. "Do you think you are fit enough to paddle back to the docks to determine the level of activity so that we can moor next to the warehouse and pinch the rifles?"

"All the way back?" O'Connell realized his comment sounded pre-cisely like what it was: A whine.

"No, Peter. Not all the way back. We can ferry you to the shipping channel and then you can paddle the rest of the way. If it is all clear, you can signal us with your torch and we will pull up to a mooring position on the quay. You sink the folboat, climb up and help us unload as many crates of rifles as this ship can carry. You can do that, right?" It was not a query. It was clearly an order.

"Yes, sir. We can do that." O'Connell looked at Barker and Barker nodded.

SEA RAIDERS

26 November 1944. Late morning,

MERCURY CORPORACAO warehouse

Steinmark returned to the warehouse after attending first Mass at Santa Catalina. He was wearing his best linen suit and the récent rain made the warehouse damp as well as almost cool. Though attendance at Mass had helped build his relationship in the community, Steinmark also was a practicing Catholic and he definitely felt better after Sunday Mass. Even with all the turmoil that he faced with the new Nazi leadership and this new mission working with the Soviets, an hour at Mass served to calm him.

Steinmark was thinking about the recent offer from Judith Connelly. She was so transparent. The "partnership" offer last night had been too direct for him not to understand she was offering a chance for him to work for the British. To be a traitor. During Mass, he decided this would be his last mission for Berlin, but he would not be a traitor to Germany. Today would be the last day he spent in Goa. It was time to leave for good.

Now, he had to face a communist who was interested in only one thing: German technology. Would the Soviets live up to their end of the bargain and help exfiltrate senior leaders? Steinmark doubted it, but he would make an effort to obey his orders one last time. He looked down at the Luger in the open desk drawer. After today, he wouldn't need that pistol any more.

He heard the Soviet officer arrive at the front door and saw him talking to his Mombasa team leader Murtaza as they walked to the office. The Soviet walked into the office and sat down while Murtaza waited at the door. Steinmark nodded to the Mombasa smuggler and spoke to him in English. "Thank you. You can leave now, Murtaza."

"Sir, I need to talk to you a moment. Please, sir. In the warehouse."

"Excuse me. There is something I have to see." The Soviet nodded and Steinmark stood up. He closed the desk drawer and walked past the Soviet toward his team leader. As he did, two rounds from a small pistol hit their mark.

O'Connell and Barker pulled under the concrete docks next to the warehouse and once again Barker climbed the ladder until his head just cleared the dock. It was still raining steadily and while afternoon, there was no sun at all under the heavy clouds. The downpour made the area look even more abandoned than it was earlier that morning. Barker climbed down the ladder and stopped so he was facing O'Connell.

"You had to show them the rifle, didn't you. Such a thorough debriefing. Now, here we are... *again,* and God only knows what we will see inside the warehouse."

"Don't be a cry baby. You are only worried about the fact that you might lose those bags of gold doubloons."

"They are English gold sovereigns and there are two for each of us. They are safe for now in my ruck. And why were you looking under my seat of the folboat?"

"Curious. I've always been curious."

"And I have always been poor. I was going to share them with you. Now, I'm not so sure."

"Gold sovereigns. A nice little nest egg if we ever get out of here."

"That's what I thought. After all, we don't know for sure when or where they were minted. Could be German counterfeit, you know. Either way, I reckon gold is gold and a bag or two, more or less, isn't going to matter to anyone at the bottom of the sea. Now, signal the trawler so we can get this done."

O'Connell climbed up the ladder to just below the concrete dock. He faced out to sea and used a red filtered flashlight to send in Morse code *CC* for clear, clear.

While waiting for the fishing boat, they pulled up Barker's kit bag which included his explosives, the small crossbow and the bags of gold. After they scuttled the folboat, the two commandos worked their way across the docks to the warehouse door.

Barker turned to O'Connell and said, "Once again, I am waiting for you to do the needful."

There was a relatively loud click as O'Connell finished picking the lock. He looked up at Barker and said, "Once again, I am on my knees completing the task. Let's go look at what's left in the warehouse."

What they saw surprised them. Empty. It was an empty warehouse, except for some packing material, a few splinters from when they had opened the boxes hours earlier. O'Connell walked over to the small office near the front of the building. The door was open.

He walked out of the office and motioned for Barker who came and looked through the windows that divided the office from the rest of the warehouse. He could see the feet and legs of a body slightly hidden behind the desk. A man in a linen suit. An eye patch on his right eye.

Barker looked over his shoulder and said, "Steinmark?"

"Looks like Steinmark. Two rounds in his chest. He is very dead." Peter continued as he pulled a pistol out from his coveralls. "He had a Luger in his hand. It appears he knew the fight was coming but didn't expect it to happen today."

"Seems like the Soviet was not interested in fulfilling his part of the bargain."

"Seems like."

Barker shook his head and said, "I'm sure they completed the transfer. He must have waved his second ship off the dock and went back in to sort out the arrangements with his Russian counterpart.

Two rounds were all he got. If I had been the Russian, I would have used a British revolver to do the necessary so that we ended up blamed."

"So, his guards are still out front?"

"Well at least one of them is still here in the warehouse." Barker pointed to a set of legs in one of the corners of the warehouse. "Also dead. The rest are probably at some bar waiting to be paid. We need to leave here before the Portuguese authorities come and visit based on an anonymous call that they will have received. Let's hope Drake and Donohue didn't dawdle."

They ran to the end of the warehouse. Now that his eyes were used to the shadows of the warehouse, O'Connell saw the African slumped in that unnatural posture that only occurs with death. After determining the African was also dead from two rounds in the back of the head, they departed via the man door, and O'Connell reset the lock. They looked down the concrete pier to see the fishing trawler pulling up at a mooring station twenty yards from the warehouse. Barker and O'Connell ran to the trawler. Donohue threw them the line to tie up the boat. Instead, they jumped on deck and insisted the trawler head back to sea.

Drake was the first to respond as the trawler slowly headed toward the shipping channel. "No guns?"

Barker said, "No, sir. No guns, no crates, nothing in the warehouse but a dead Steinmark and a member of his pirate clan."

"Also dead?"

O'Connell responded, "Very dead."

Donohue looked at O'Connell. "Your doing?"

"No, sir. We reckon probably his Russian partner in this effort, but honestly, we have no idea other than the fact that he received two bullets in the chest."

Barker took over and said, "There's a chance it was his pirate colleagues, but I don't see why they would double cross their boss and, if they did, it would probably have been a knife in the chest not bullets. Still, pirates are really just mercenaries, so maybe the Russian outbid the Nazi."

Drake had been at a slow simmer throughout this discussion and he finally boiled over. "You can't imagine a Kenyan or an Indonesian or Indians associated with a Nazi might want sophisticated German rifles? A lack of imagination, Barker. For their future efforts against the Empire, no doubt." "Sir, if that is the case, then it is all for the good that we have explosive charges set on the crates, don't you think?"

Drake looked at Donohue and shook his head. He was used to a fair degree of insubordination from SOE operators who were not regular Army or Navy and he couldn't honestly see the point in arguing with Barker.

O'Connell broke the silence. "Sir, if you want to intercept the ships, we probably have time. Assuming they intend to transfer the entire lot to some Soviet, German or local cargo hauler, we can expect that would take place after dark, no? Do you still have your MTB handy?"

Donohue nodded and said, "That's why we brought you along O'Connell. Not just a blunt instrument. Some brains in that paratrooper head of yours as well." He looked at Drake and said, "We have a radio on board. Once we clear Goan waters, we can transfer to the MTB and we could indeed intercept the ships at sea." Drake nodded and Donohue climbed the ladder to the pilot house and spoke to Mohammed and the skipper of the trawler. Below decks, they felt the change of course and heard the old engine in the trawler begin to apply more power to the ancient screws.

As the trawler pulled past the harbor buoys, Barker pointed back to the docks and shouted, "My incendiaries seem to have started working." The entire MERCURY CORPORACAO warehouse was in flames.

"Good riddance," was all O'Connell had to say as they headed out to sea.

The trawler met the MTB in the shipping channel just outside the sovereign limits of Portuguese authority. The sun was setting and turned the clouds to the West a brilliant orange. The storm was over and the sea had quieted to a steady chop. In the planning discussions before the linkup with the MTB, Drake ordered Kelly to return to her warehouse via the trawler, sanitize any sign of SOE involvement in the warehouse and her apartment and then return immediately to India. Donohue offered Mohammed as Kelly's guardian angel and she accepted. There was a brief moment on the deck after the final discussions when O'Connell and Kelly were alone. He took her hands in his and said, "I will be coming back to see you when we are all through with this."

Kelly smiled, "As they say in your American movies, I will be waiting. Meanwhile, please keep that Irish-American head attached to the Irish-American body. I've grown quite attached to both."

Barker called from the deck of the MTB. "O'Connell, are you coming or staying?"

O'Connell nodded, caught a quick, first kiss from Kelly and jumped on the MTB. He had barely landed on the deck of the Royal Navy craft when they accelerated at full throttle.

O'Connell's experience in naval vessels had been limited to his exfiltration by US Navy submarine after the Italian resistance delivered their wounded American to the coast. That trip had been remarkably short and mostly under water. As a child, he watched speed boat races along the Niagara River near Buffalo. Now, here he was traveling at 25 knots, in the dark, and bouncing like a pinball. The ship's commander, a young Royal Navy Lieutenant named Palmer, tried to balance maximizing his speed while dodging the various sea buoys that the Portuguese had placed on the outer reaches of their colonial territory. It was definitely not as fun as it looked in the war newsreels of PT boats in the Pacific.

"O'Connell, you need to brace yourself against something or you will be covered in bruises well before we board the Steinmark vessels." Donohue seemed to be actually enjoying the ride and he offered

O'Connell a hand up to the armor plated station next to the port side twin .50 machine gun mount.

"Son, I know you tried to do the right thing in the warehouse," Donohue said. "Drake is a good man, but he remains a loyal member of the British Commonwealth. While I don't harbor any ill feelings toward our allies, sometimes it really does appear that Standish is right and SEAC, doesn't really stand for South East Asia Command, it stands for Save European Allies Colonies. Still, it was disappointing to find the weapons gone."

O'Connell pushed a fresh wash of sea spray from his eyes and said, "Sir, it's really quite simple. There were crates of these weapons. It wasn't as if we could have carried a crate of weapons in the folboat. It was more than a little awkward just carrying one inside the canvas hull."

"Of course, son. So, now we have to try to intercept them to ensure they don't end up in hands of ne'er-do-wells. I hope you are ready for some piracy on the high seas."

"I saw the MTB contingent preparing a boarding party. I think I will be best served following their lead rather than taking the lead. I've never been at sea in a fast boat like this."

Donohue tried, unsuccessfully to light a cigarette behind the armored plate. O'Connell reached over and used his Zippo lighter to light it. When he came back to face O'Connell he said, "Wise choice, son. Underway operations are never as easy as it looks in the movies. That was my experience in the last war."

The second in command, an ensign named Bograth who looked to O'Connell to be about twelve years old approached Donohue. "Skipper wants to see you and Commander Drake in the chart room."

Donohue turned to O'Connell and said, "Wait here and try not to create too much of a fuss, please." O'Connell nodded to Donohue just as another bit of salt spray flooded his left ear.

The "chart room" was nothing more than a small room below deck which served as the navigator's chart storage, the mess table and, based on the smell, probably the table used for weapons cleaning. Lieutenant Palmer was already talking to Commander Drake. The cabin was dimly lit with red filtered lights and a single red light pulled close to a chart. Drake had taken the opportunity to light his pipe, so Donohue pulled out his cigarette holder and cigarettes and lit one for himself.

"Patrick, according to the young lieutenant, we are approaching our prey. This MTB has one of the new radar sets and it shows two ships of about the right size anchored side by side. There is no reason for them to be out here. It isn't a shipping channel and certainly nowhere near an anchorage for ships waiting for a pilot boat into Goa. He has already slowed the boat and shifted to a muffler system to let us to creep up on the ships. If we identify them as our candidates, we can certainly board them one at a time."

"John, do you and the Lieutenant think we have enough men on board to take over one or both of the ships?"

Lieutenant Palmer said, "Sir, my men are well trained as a boarding party. I think we can gain control of at least one of the ships. We are counting on surprise and a good chance that most of the crew won't put up a fight when they see us boarding. It might be a little chancy if they are flying the Portuguese flag, but that's not something we will know until we get near enough to board. I will leave it to you to sort out the cargo."

Drake replied, "Best do, Lieutenant. We have to demobilize some explosives that were placed on the cargo to ensure they didn't fall into the wrong hands."

"Sir, what is the risk to my boat?"

"None, Lieutenant so long as we are the ones involved with the cargo." Drake looked up at Donohue. They both knew that time pencil detonators were not precise and, honestly, the devices could explode at any time though they were supposed to explode after midnight. That fell into the category of "need to know" and a Royal Navy lieutenant did not need to know.

Before they could decide if they wanted the lieutenant to know more, the ensign came into the room. "Sir, we have another craft on the radar. It looks to be a submarine, a very large submarine and not in any of our books." The Lieutenant looked at his two passengers and said, "Well, gentlemen, I think that changes everything unless you have also called in a Royal Navy submarine."

"Not a chance, Lieutenant. Also, you must assume the submarine is a hostile."

"Aye aye, sir. We know how to approach hostiles in these waters." The Lieutenant was the first up the ladder to the deck shouting orders as he went.

Patrick had the cigarette holder between his teeth in a pose reminiscent of the US President. He asked, "John, what now?"

"Patrick, I have no idea at this point." Drake looked at his watch. It was 1922hrs. Plenty of time for night action before the charges exploded. Maybe. "We will certainly find out soon enough." He turned and climbed up the short ladder to the deck. As Donohue climbed the ladder, the MTB made a sharp turn to starboard and accelerated.

O'Connell reached out to Donohue as soon as he came on deck. "Sir, what's going on? The Lieutenant comes up the ladder yelling "Action Stations" and suddenly his team are donning helmets and manning the guns and the torpedo tubes."

"Submarine on the surface approaching the two ships, son. I don't know who is going to fire first, but I suspect we will be in a fight sooner than we thought. As a Navy officer, admittedly a reserve Navy officer, I recommend for now we stay out of the way." The MTB began a long, curved course change. Previously, it had been heading almost due West, to approach the anchored vessels from the stern. Now, they had turned North and away from the vessels. It didn't take a nautical mind to determine the new plan was to approach the submarine and the two cargo ships from the north while the crews were busy transferring cargo.

Barker struggled to come over to O'Connell and yelled in his right ear. "You reckon we have a place in this game of action stations?"

O'Connell shrugged and said, "I doubt our pistols or this new German rifle are going to have any role in this fight. I am trying to figure out where the most armor is located so that when the fight does start, I have a place to hide."

"Peter, you are singing my tune. I reckon it is behind either the port or starboard gun mounts. There are two layers of armor covering that position. And, because if the gunner is wounded, we might join the fight by manning the guns. Meanwhile, I picked up a spare set of Navy binoculars so maybe we can sort out what is going to happen."

Barker leaned over the turret of the gun mount and away from the gunner and the loader preparing the twin .50 caliber machine guns for action. He braced against the turret in an effort to see what was ahead of them in the tossing and now turning boat. "There is an enormous submarine about a mile ahead of us, on the surface. Looks twice the size of any Allied sub I have ever seen. The crew are inflating large semi-rigid rafts. It looks like there is a gun crew…". The first round from the submarine's deck gun landed 25 yards to their front and about 10 yards to their starboard side. Lieutenant Palmer spun the wheel of the MTB toward the spray caused by the round. "What is he doing?" Barker yelled to no one in particular. He hadn't noticed that Drake was behind him.

"Barker, I commanded a four-stack destroyer in the last war when I was about as young as our lieutenant. One way to out-fox someone with a deck gun is to move faster than he can adjust fire. I suspect by the time we reach where the last round hit…"

The second round from the deck gun landed aft of the MTB and near enough to their previous position that Barker said, "Understood, sir. He responds to the rounds and hopes that eventually he will be able to line up to send a couple of torpedoes on their way."

"Exactly so, Barker. Exactly so. Now, our job is to stay out of his way and out of the way of the crew. They know what they are doing even in the dark and we can't help. Why don't you join me next to the starboard gun. O'Connell, I think you should stay with your commander next to the port gun position. We may have some utility eventually, but for now, I just want us clear of the action."

As experienced officers, Drake and Donohue exhibited a level of battlefield calm that O'Connell had seen in Italy with Commander Sciandretti. Sciandretti had been in more than a dozen firefights when O'Connell arrived as a young OSS officer. He seemed to know in advance what was going to happen and therefore, his orders were direct, precise, and without any rush. O'Connell didn't have any idea what he should do on this MTB, so he followed Drake's instructions and stumbled across the wet and pitching deck to the port gun position. There he found Donohue sitting with his back to the gun position, puffing away on a cigarette.

"Good to see you, son. Take a seat and let the Royal Navy do her job. Just a quick question: Do you know how to fire a set of twin .50 caliber machine guns? I do not. My experience with Naval gunfire is with far larger weapons. I hope we don't have to learn on the job."

"Sir, the M2 is a friend from the United States Army. A pair of M2s are just double the fun. I got that under control if we have to take a part in the game. I can show you the loader job in about 10 seconds. Of course, I don't know if I can hit anything in this rocking horse of a boat, but that is another story."

O'Connell heard the sound of rounds hitting the armor plate on the gun position above his head. They were obviously closing in on the submarine and the crew decided to use the machine guns positioned on the sail of the submarine as well as the deck gun. In response again, Palmer turned the boat to port so hard that the bow wave washed along the deck behind the gun position.

As they turned, O'Connell could see the trawlers for the first time. Still a half mile out, but clearly visible. The muzzle flashes from the deck of the trawlers argued that they intended to join the fight along with their submarine mates. They were wasting their ammunition trying to hit the MTB, but no one said they were well trained. As the MTB closed to effective range, the starboard gun position opened up the twin .50s on the shooters on the deck of the trawler. O'Connell couldn't tell for sure in the darkness, but it looked like the port gunner also had run tracer rounds along the entire deck of the trawler. Donohue said to O'Connell, "That should dissuade them from any further hostilities."

The MTB passed behind the first ship just as they heard what could only be described as the sound of a giant hammer hitting plate steel. The ship almost immediately began to list to port and its twin engine stacks and the deck crane hit the deck of their partner ship. A second sound, this time clearly a larger explosion, came from the open cargo hold of the stricken ship. A flash of flame erupted from the cargo hold at a height above the cargo crane. This explosion seemed to break the keel of the ship precisely at the cargo hold. The bow and the stern began to rise up from the sea to meet in a crushing noise as the crew dove into the water and began to swim to the second ship. Most made it to the cargo net, some did not.

O'Connell looked at his watch. It was 2025hrs. He turned to Donohue and shouted, "Sir, It would appear the SOE time pencils are not quite as precise as advertised."

Donohue nodded and said, "I'm not going to complain."

Throughout the gunfight, the second ship had been off-loading their cargo onto the rigid hulled boats from the submarine and crates were being loaded by a small crane on the submarine's deck into an open cargo hatch forward of the conning tower. As the MTB swung below the stern of the remaining cargo ship, the crew once again opened fire on the Royal Navy craft. Steady bursts from both sets of twin .50s settled the argument quickly. Once the threat from the cargo ship was eliminated, the MTB skipper turned his boat in another long arc so that the MTB was now on the opposite side and running a perpendicular track to the submarine. The MTB torpedomen were working on arming their weapons and preparing the air compressors used to launch their "fish."

It was up to Palmer to align the boat and judge the distance. The crew of the submarine clearly understood the threat and reengaged the MTB with their deck gun and machine guns on the sail as the MTB came within range. As soon as they did, both port and starboard twin .50 positions opened up. The MTB rattled from both the rounds from the submarine hitting the deck and from the hundreds of expended cases from the twin .50s. Before Palmer could complete his maneuver for the torpedo run, there came an explosion from one of the rigid hull boats tied up next to the submarine. Shortly after that, another boat adjacent to the submarine also exploded with much greater force. Since both blasts took place on the far side of the submarine, the MTB crew could not see if the submarine was damaged. But, in the flash of the explosions, they did have chance to see the giant silhouette of the cargo submarine.

After the flash, they saw the submarine suddenly start underway at a high speed with the crew working frantically to close all hatches and dive. By the time the MTB was lined up for a proper torpedo run, all that was visible of the submarine as the top of the sail, the periscope and a two pair of snorkels. One pair obviously providing air for the crew and the engines and one pair for the diesel exhaust. The second pair of snorkels was belching black smoke as the diesel engines were pressed to full power. Just before the sail disappeared below the surface, both Drake and Donohue noted that painted in red on the top of the submarine's tower were a hammer and sickle and the number 237. The submarine quickly slipped below the waves with only the exhaust stacks of the diesel engines above water and disappeared into the night leaving only the smell of diesel exhaust.

The MTB came to a halt as Palmer pulled the throttles to all stop. He looked over at Drake and Donohue as the two intelligence officers stood up at the end of the firefight. "I thought there was no threat to my boat from the cargo?"

Drake gave the lieutenant his most serious face, pulled his still smoking pipe from his mouth and said, "Lieutenant, if you have a question for my colleague, you may address him as Commander Donohue. You may address me either as Sir or as Commander Drake when you have a question." The Lieutenant stopped as if he had been slapped in the face.

Drake continued, "There was no threat to your boat. You saw the explosions yourself, they were nearly a half hour after we would have boarded and rendered safe any explosives. If there had been no action from the submarine, it should have been an easy boarding party effort. The crews of the cargo ships and the submarine decided to fight, and they paid for their actions. Now, are you ready to continue this mission or do we need to call in another Royal Navy vessel?" Drake did not wait for Lieutenant Palmer to answer. He turned to Barker and whispered, "Are all of your little widgets accounted for, Barker?"

Barker nodded and said, "All present and correct, sir. Two placed, two exploded…though a bit early. I suspect the last explosion was some sort of sympathetic detonation caused by rounds from the twin .50s or shrapnel from the other explosion. One of the crates had *panzerfaust* anti-tank rockets."

Drake looked down at the SOE operator still sitting behind the starboard machine gun turret, smiled and said, "Excellent. Then you won't mind joining the boarding party on the remaining ship."

Barker stood up and said, "No sir. I'm not worried at all and will be happy to join the Royal Navy."

T he boarding party detained the crew and took control of the ship. Barker made a quick inspection of all the cargo and O'Connell helped the boarding party detain Steinmark's mix of Malaysians and Kenyans. Ensign Bograth took command of his first ship, a "prize vessel" in Royal Navy terms. He and his small boarding party headed north to Bombay followed by the MTB. By mid-day on 27 November, the MTB and the cargo ship were in Royal Navy berths and Palmer, Bograth and the MTB crew were the toast of the Royal Navy Lines. They were, after all, one of the few crews in harbor who had actually boarded an enemy ship. They were also the only crew in the harbor who were going to receive compensation for the prize vessel. The SOE and OSS team disappeared well before anyone knew they were even on the docks. Before they left, Drake used his local connections to arrange for the cargo to be transferred to a small warehouse on the docks and passed the handling of the "prize crew" to British Special Branch personnel.

On 29 November, Drake and Barker met at Donohue's bungalow to provide further updates. Drake was clearly pleased with the results. After raising whiskey glasses in a toast to the success of OPERATION DILLETANTE, Drake said, "I received an interim report from Special Branch today. Honestly, it was passed with a grumble, but they couldn't argue about our success. The initial interrogation did not go all that well. They were able to determine that the crew was a mix of

Malaysians, Indonesians and some sailors, well actually pirates, from the port of Mombasa. Once they were informed their paymaster, Traumann, was dead -- and, I suspect, after they were threatened with being hung by the Royal Navy, -- they offered their side of the story." Drake paused to take a sip from his drink. "It appears that they were only part of a larger program by Steinmark. Three of the crew were aware that Steinmark was a Nazi and he had promised them good pay, in English gold sovereigns no less!" O'Connell had to force himself to avoid looking at Barker.

Drake continued, "They were all willing to help the Nazi in his smuggling efforts because he also promised them a future free from both British and, in the case of the Indonesians, Dutch authority. What really caught the Special Branch interest was that some of the Mombasa pirates had been involved in launching and recovering members of the sabotage circuit Steinmark ran in Bombay. They didn't know much about the identities of the individuals, but they did know the saboteurs were from a Hindu criminal gang led by a man named Golpani. It changed the Special Branch investigation completely. They were looking for members of the Indian independence movement as targets of their investigation on sabotage on the docks. Now they have leads that they can use to find the real villains. I have to admit it is the first time that Force 136 has received a formal letter of thanks from the Raj. Hard to say if that is a good thing or a bad thing. It might ruin our reputation as members of the Ministry of Ungentlemanly Warfare. I will come back to that shortly."

Drake briefly explained that the cargo was delivered to a technology intelligence unit known as T-Force. T-Force was responsible collecting information on enemy advanced technology and what they refer to as Nazi "super weapons." They reported to Drake that the documents on the aircraft engines were most interesting. They described the design and capability of a fighter aircraft attacking the allied air force squadrons over Germany. The Messerschmidt ME-262 or "Swallow" aircraft has two of these engines. This fighter is the fastest combat aircraft in Europe right now and the capture of the operational manuals promised to advance T-Force understanding of the technology.

Donohue returned to Drake's previous comment on reputation. He asked, "You said there was some additional question of our role in ungentlemanly warfare?"

Drake smiled, "Sad to say, our young Navy lieutenant decided to be completely truthful to his Navy superiors when he was debriefed. His truthfulness included statements noting that we did not explain how we knew the ships were there nor did we identify whether the cargo ships were flying Nazi or Japanese ensigns. Further, he noted that the submarine we engaged was identified tentatively as a Soviet vessel, apparently a captured Nazi Type X transport submarine. I have received a number of different requests from the Royal Navy in Bombay to explain our reasons for asking the young lieutenant and his ship to conduct operations on the high seas that were outside the bounds of what they call normal fleet operations."

Donohue raised his glass and said, "Here's to abnormal fleet operations!"

Drake chuckled, "Of course, the Fleet is not going to press any charges against the lieutenant because of the significant successes and, they pointed out, because the inspection of the ship did find a Nazi Navy ensign in the communications room. I did not tell my fleet counterparts that I liberated a Portuguese flag and a British Merchant Marine flag from the same compartment before they inspected the ship."

O'Connell couldn't restrain himself, "Did they decide what to make of the Soviet submarine taking on Nazi technology and shooting at the MTB?"

Drake shook his head and said, "I think the Royal Navy board of inquiry decided it was too complicated for them to address. After all, they didn't have anything other than Lieutenant Palmer's report to confirm the livery on the submarine's sail which was inconsistent with his identification of the submarine as a Nazi Type X cargo craft.

I wasn't about to provide any report at all to the Navy given the fact that DILETTANTE was our secret little operation." Drake turned to Donohue and asked, "Have they reached out to you, Patrick?"

"A number of colleagues from the Indian Government have reached out to me to determine what role I might have had in the entire adventure. I told them the same thing I always say: I am merely a simple US Navy Reserve commander who served in the Great War and is now responsible for transferring OSS officers from Bombay to our joint forces in Kandy and Calcutta. If there was a successful operation at sea, clearly that would have been outside my remit. I did offer my congratulations to the Royal Navy when I recently visited the Bombay Yacht Club."

Drake answered, "I think it is time for you to do the needful and make O'Connell's transfer as soon as possible. I will be doing the same for my man Barker. The sooner our malefactors leave the scene of the crime, the better, no?"

Barker finally spoke up and said, "Sir, I will be happy to raise a toast for that action."

Later that afternoon, Drake and Donohue went to another room to "plot and plan" as they said to their junior officers. Alone with O'Connell, Barker raised another toast. "It would appear that all of the gold went down with the second ship," he said. "Our little nest egg will have to be set aside for a few years, just in case."

"Well, if the Royal Navy can issue prize money for their sea raiders, it only seems right that we would receive some fair compensation."

"After all, we still don't know how Steinmark acquired the gold."

"And we still have a war to fight, Clive, so it hardly matters. My only recommendation is that you find someplace safe to store it. Hard to carry sacks of gold around in the jungles of Burma. It would be mighty tempting for a Burmese resistance fighter to ensure we didn't make it back."

Barker put the forefinger of his right hand on the side of his nose and said, "I already thought of that, mate, and have enlisted a trusted colleague who, I promise, will not give up our secret."

"Judith?"

"One and the same. She is now stationed here in Bombay as a dispatcher for SOE agents headed into Burma and China. I figured she could keep our booty in her apartment until we returned. If we don't make it back, then she can do anything she wants with it. She earned her share in this adventure and, as you said, if the Royal Navy sailors can be rewarded for a "prize ship" captured in the heat of battle, I reckon a little gold for us is small compensation."

"Clive, you are a pirate at heart."

"O'Connell, you come from a tribe of reivers and ship breakers. You can't really think piracy is all that bad a profession."

>>>>>> **EPILOGUE**

10 November 1945

Peter O'Connell and Clive Barker returned from Southeast Asia in late October 1945.

As originally planned, Barker spent the last year of the war in Malaysia with Force 136. O'Connell had expected to join Detachment 101 in Burma. Instead, as part of Detachment 404, he ended up working in French Indo-China and then with the Free Thai resistance units. Near the war's end, he moved into Bangkok to help manage the surrender of Japanese forces in Siam and to help in liberating Allied prisoners of war from Japanese internment camps.

It was far less dangerous than VIGNETTE, CRANKCASE, or DILETTANTE, but O'Connell was fascinated with the Thai and the Northern tribes of the Shan and Kachin as well as Hmong tribesmen on the Siam-Lao border. Once again, he realized that the most effective resistance against the Japanese came from men who claimed to be communists. Again, not the most popular message among SEAC leadership. Det 404 leadership didn't give a damn about politics. Their task was to defeat the Japanese and, once that was accomplished, find Allies in POW camps throughout Siam and Indo-China. When the French colonial troops started arriving, the OSS teams returned to Calcutta. For his work in Siam, O'Connell received a Legion of Merit medal and promotion to Lieutenant Colonel. But, by the time he arrived in Bombay, the OSS no longer existed. LTC Peter O'Connell was an unassigned Army officer and no supporting military unit.

This meant that his return to the United States was delayed as units with real commanders took precedence on troop ships heading home. Conventional Army leadership wanted nothing to do with the OSS veterans and the only way for someone like O'Connell to return home was to either wait at the end of the line or, ideally, grab a sling seat on one of the remaining Carpetbagger aircraft.

During the delay, Peter Gareth O'Connell of Buffalo, NY and Judith Mary Margaret Kelly of the city of Armagh, Northern Ireland married at the Gloria Church inside the Bombay Royal Navy Lines. The OSS and SOE agents decided to have the wedding as soon as they could so that they could return to the US together. The Royal Navy helped as did the US mission in New Delhi. They held their service one day before the annual Remembrance Day ceremony held inside the Navy Lines in Bombay. The small colonial Catholic church filled with a gathering of SOE and OSS operators from the CBI as well as a number of Royal Navy personnel. Recently promoted Royal Navy Captain John Drake gave away the bride and Lieutenant Colonel Clive Barker served as O'Connell's best man.

With the SOE and the OSS disbanded, Drake returned to his fleet responsibilities in the Office of Naval Intelligence. Barker, like O'Connell, was an officer without a supporting military unit. He was waiting his turn to return to England. OSS/Bombay Detachment Commander Donohue maintained his US Navy reserve commission awaiting his demobilization orders. Donohue and Mohammed Shir Wazir were honored guests and they hosted the formal dinner after the ceremony at the compound on Malabar Hill. Donohue wore his Navy White Mess uniform. It was the first and only time that O'Connell saw him in uniform. O'Connell did notice at the top row of Donohue's ribbons included a Navy Cross and a Purple Heart. Mohammed wore a South Waziristan Scouts mess dress uniform showing him to be a Color Sergeant in the Scouts. He wore three rows of ribbons that O'Connell couldn't decipher and stitched to the right shoulder of his mess jacket was an embroidered set of SOE wings. A combat jump with SOE? The tales of Donohue and Mohammed's adventures would have to be told some other time or, O'Connell realized, perhaps never.

Christmas Day, 1945 Luanda, Portuguese West Africa

Gilberto Tambao walked out from Christmas Mass at the Cathedral of the Holy Savior. The Portuguese community in Luanda was about to spend a day of celebration and Tambao intended to join as many of the small parties of the Portuguese elite as he could before the day was out. This was his first Christmas in Luanda and as a formal patron of the Cathedral. His name was well known in the community as a philanthropist and the owner of a small import business focused on the delivery of oil exploration equipment from the United States by way of Brazil. The end of the World War had brought opportunities to Portuguese businessmen who were willing to leave the homeland and work in a colony.

The members of the Luanda Yacht Club and the Luanda business community admired Tambao's ability to balance work with pleasure. The well-dressed man with his rakish looks advanced by his black silk eyepatch was a regular at the horse races and the Yacht Club. His looks, his style and his interests in art and jazz music made him even more attractive to the ladies in the colony. To his closest colleagues, he attributed this commitment to both business and what he called "the good life" to his experiences as a young man in oil and mining exploration in Brazil and his most recent work in Mozambique.

"I lost an eye working to make my fortune in mining in Brazil in the 1930s. Then, I nearly lost that same fortune in the 1940s in investments in the colony in Mozambique. One never knows when something bad is going to happen in life and I don't intend to waste another minute." When he was asked about the accident that cost him his eye, Tambao answered philosophically, "An explosion gone bad. It was my own fault since I was carrying the explosives. But, I suppose the loss made me the person I am today."

By the time Tambao returned home after a day of visiting friends at Christmas celebrations, his servants had already filled a bathtub with cool water and laid out his sailing clothes. It was his habit to spend at least one night a month on his motor yacht and tonight was perfect because of the fireworks at the harbor. After he dressed, he filled a small overnight bag with a change of clothes, two bottles of his favorite Portuguese wines, and a bottle of expensive port from the home country. His driver was waiting in the driveway. They left in his newly imported American convertible and arrived at the harbor just before the horizon turned from gold to deep blue. Before he walked to his yacht, he stopped at the harbor master's office and delivered the bottle of port as a Christmas present.

Two hours later, Tambao was sitting on the deck of his yacht drinking white wine recently chilled in the harbor water and eating from a bowl of olives. A voice in Spanish came up from the dock, "May I come aboard?"

A puzzled Tambao looked at the luminous dial on his Italian diver's watch and used his left hand to reach into his bag and pull out his Mauser pistol. He responded back in Spanish, "You are welcome to come aboard."

As the visitor came aboard, Tambao noticed the visitor was walking with a familiar limp. "Klaus?"

The visitor spoke softly and in German, "Jan, the name is Pedro now. I hope all is well."

"All is well, old comrade, for a man named Tambao. Most especially when the ballast on his boat is made of gold."

J.R. SEEGER is a western New York native who served as a U.S. Army paratrooper and as a CIA case officer for a total of 27 years of federal service. In October 2001, Mr. Seeger led a CIA paramilitary team into Afghanistan. He splits his time between western New York and Central New Mexico.

Made in the USA
San Bernardino, CA
25 March 2020